The Voice at the Door

A NOVEL OF EMILY DICKINSON

The Voice
at the Door

A NOVEL OF EMILY DICKINSON

JAMES SULZER

PUBLISHING

Ashland, Oregon

Fuze Publishing
2305-C Ashland Street, #312
Ashland, OR 97520

Book design by Ray Rhamey
Author photograpy by Laurie Richards

ISBN 978-0-9897306-2-4

Library of Congress Control Number: 2013947653

For Barbara,
again and always

INTRODUCTION

They say every family has its eccentric. In my family it was Uncle William Norcross. He was a doctor, an expert on infectious disease who made a quiet living as a consultant to charitable organizations. Later in life after the death of his wife, and a subsequent failed romance, he moved to Amherst, Massachusetts—the home of his lifelong obsession, the poet Emily Dickinson.

For the last twenty-two years of his life, William rented a tiny apartment in the tower of a Victorian house not far from the Dickinson Homestead.

There he disappeared from public view for weeks at a time. He dropped hints that he was working on a manuscript of earth-shaking importance, but I never quite believed him. He was a medical man, not a writer, I thought.

Over the years, based on his extensive research, he devised some novel theories about Emily Dickinson's withdrawal from the world and a long distance love affair with a married man, all of which—according to William—prompted some of her most extraordinary poetry. He must have known that his ideas would astound some and dismay others.

There were also stories during those years that a wraith-like figure, clad all in white, sometimes drifted about Amherst in the early hours before dawn, and some connected William with its appearance, though that was never substantiated. Once, indeed, the figure was said to enter the little bakery close to the Dickinson homestead, and a message chalked itself on the daily menu board: *Graham bread today, ½ gill of lard.* Rumors and hearsay, probably.

Upon my uncle's death the following manuscript was discovered among his papers. At first I couldn't take his hypothesis seriously, but as I read on, I came to know and understand an Emily Dickinson who was altogether new and endearing. I saw how her upbringing contributed to her reclusiveness, how her sly sense of humor developed in the give and take of family interactions, and how her ecstasy and despair were opposite sides of the same coin. Her beautiful but enigmatic poems seemed, suddenly, more human and approachable; and for the first time I felt I understood the love and the pain that were so much a part of her poetry.

William's manuscript is now in your hands. I hope you will give his life's work the care and attention that I believe it deserves.

Sincerely,

James Sulzer,
Nephew and Executor

Timeline of Emily Dickinson's life

1813

Samuel Fowler Dickinson (grandfather) builds the Homestead on Main Street.

1828, May 6

Edward Dickinson (father) and Emily Norcross (mother) marry.

1829, April 16

William Austin Dickinson (Austin), Emily's brother, is born.

1830, December 10

Emily Elizabeth Dickinson is born.

1833, February 28

Lavinia Dickinson (Vinnie), Emily's sister is born.

1833, March

Under financial pressure because of possible mismanagement of his affairs, Samuel Fowler Dickinson sells the Homestead; the family continues to rent and live in east half of the house.

1840, April

Edward Dickinson, his wife, and their three children move to the house on West Street (now called North Pleasant Street).

1847, September – 1848, August

Emily attends Mount Holyoke Female Seminary.

1850, Summer

Austin begins to court Emily's friend Susan Gilbert.

1855, February

Emily and Vinnie visit Father in Washington, DC.

1855, March

The sisters visit Eliza Coleman in Philadelphia, where Emily meets the Reverend Charles Wadsworth.

1855, November

Having repurchased it a year earlier, Edward Dickinson and family (including Emily) move back to the Homestead.

1856, July

Austin marries Susan Gilbert; they move to the "Evergreens" next door to the Homestead.

1860, Summer

Charles Wadsworth visits Emily at the Homestead.

1860, October 19

Emily and Vinnie visit Eliza in Middletown, CT.

1862, May

Charles Wadsworth and family move to San Francisco, where he is installed at Calvary Presbyterian Church.

1864, April – November and 1865, April – October

Emily receives treatment for her eyes in Boston, living in Cambridge with her cousins Louisa and Fanny Norcross.

1869, July

Charles Wadsworth and family return to Philadelphia.

1874, June 16

Edward Dickinson (Father) dies.

1880, Summer

Charles Wadsworth visits Emily at the Homestead.

1882, April 1

Charles Wadsworth dies.

1882, September

Austin begins his affair with Mabel Loomis Todd.

1882, November 14

Emily Norcross Dickinson (Mother) dies.

1883, October 5

Thomas Gilbert Dickinson (Gib, Austin's youngest child) dies.

1886, May 15

Emily Elizabeth Dickinson dies.

PROLOGUE

Late Winter, 1855

With surprising strength for someone so slight, Emily Dickinson pulls open the door to the stove, stirs the coals with a poker, feeds more wood onto the fire, closes the door, and adjusts the vents to bank the fire. There is the satisfying clank of iron on iron as she works. As she does every morning, she prepares to bake the bread. She sets a pan of water on the stove, takes out her glass measuring cup from the cupboard and her silver measuring spoons from the drawer—both items are strictly off-limits to anyone else—and drags out the bags of corn meal and rye from the pantry.

With deft, capable hands she measures twelve cups of corn meal and twelve cups of rye into separate bowls. Turning the corn meal into a bread pan, she dashes salt upon it and pours hot water over it, stirring it with one of her silver spoons. She places it to the side to let it cool and brews herself a cup of tea. Occasionally, she jots down a line or two of verse on the back of a scrap of paper, but she reserves the evenings and nights for her more serious attempts at poetry.

Once the corn meal has cooled, she pours in the rye, adds half a cup of yeast, and dribbles in a little more water, leaving it almost too stiff to knead. She will let it stand for an hour and a half. She knows she still needs to skim the milk in the pantry and wash the remainders of last night's dishes, but first she invites Carlo, her Newfoundland dog, whose head reaches her elbow, to step outside with her. Behind a lacework of dark trees, the eastern sky is beaten gold; she can smell dew upon the grass.

As the canine lumbers off into the woods, she turns her attention to the visitor before her: a bird coming down the walk. It takes two quick hops onto the grass, turns its head sidewise as if listening for something, and plunges its beak into the moist earth. Dragging an angleworm back onto the walk, it bites it in two and gulps it down. It glances rapidly about, and for the first time it sees her. There is a look in its eye that she has noticed before; a look she often sees in birds; a look that others must have seen, too, but she knows that no one has ever captured it in words.

A sweet pain of hope and promise rises in her. She knows that words can maybe, somehow, deliver her.

A Bird, came down the Walk —
He did not know I saw —

He bit an Angle Worm in halves
And ate the fellow, raw.

She calls to Carlo, and the two of them return to the
kitchen, where she busies herself again in work. Carlo
worries his way to comfort in his old blanket and falls
back asleep.

By now it is almost eight. Her parents will soon
cease their snoring, and her sister Vinnie will give voice
to the first of her many complaints against the world.
Her brother Austin will be completing his grooming
and dressing, as he prepares to resume his courtship
of Susan Gilbert. And soon Margaret, the serving girl,
will arrive.

It is time to knead the dough.

It isn't until she is up to her elbows in its satisfying bulk that she pictures again the bird's eyes glancing
about, and the words take shape in her mind.

They looked like frightened beads.

It is the sort of impossibility that delights her.

She pauses a moment, setting the phrase in her
mind. She knows that no one, no one in the long history of the Earth, has ever seen it just this way. No one
has ever put into words, so simply and so strangely, the
look in the eyes of a bird. She knows that this is a gift.

He glanced with rapid eyes,
That hurried all abroad –
They looked like frightened Beads, I thought.

And she knows that there is no one in her life now,

no one imaginable, with whom she can share this gift. No one who can share, or understand, or love what she has been given. But her longing is unmistakable, unshakable; she is ready to entwine her heart with her intellectual equal . . . if there be such a person . . .

At dawn, in the New England winter, the trees hold out their bare hands toward the beauty of the East. And through the kitchen window, Emily Dickinson watches a bird unroll its feathers and take flight into the silver dome of heaven.

It is here that our story begins.

Part I

I had been hungry, all the Years –
My Noon had Come – to dine –

ONE

Spring, 1855

Emily doesn't know why, but she feels both highly expectant and curiously calm. She is about to meet one of the most important pastoral figures of the time. It is March of 1855, and she and her sister Vinnie are on the journey home to Amherst, Massachusetts from Washington, DC—where they have observed Father sitting in Congress. They plan to stop for a short visit in Philadelphia, where Emily's childhood friend, Eliza Coleman, has lived for several years. Often in her letters Eliza has mentioned the esteemed Charles Wadsworth.

He is an older man, married and much revered; the Colemans are his friends and parishioners. His reputation and his church have been steadily growing. The Sunday after the sisters arrive, Eliza brings them with her to hear him preach.

The Arch Street Presbyterian Church is a large brick structure much in the same style as Boston's Faneuil

Hall—a building that Emily has seen on her two trips to Boston. It is nicely proportioned and has the added beauty of marble steps and a tall stone bell tower. The meeting hall inside the church holds several hundred people, and today they pack the pews—built of chestnut fitted with newly finished red velvet seat covers. The Colemans' is near the front of the church and to the left.

A door to the side of the pulpit is thrown open and a man strides into the room.

He is moderately tall and powerfully built, and beneath his robes his bearing is erect as a soldier's. Except on top, where he is balding, his hair is long, thick, and brown. His face carries an expression that Emily has never seen before—a dignity, a seriousness, almost a grimness, and yet an underlying humor that somehow marks him as a man of great intelligence. To this day the most majestic man Emily has ever seen is her father, Edward, but Charles Wadsworth is more weighty somehow, more a man to be reckoned with. He gives the impression of having seen most of what there is to see of the world, of having understood it in its essentials, and of knowing what to value and what to dismiss.

His voice is powerful and low-pitched, yet distinct and, at the same time, smooth and lovely. "Today's sermon is on self-knowledge," he says, "something with which we all can use some assistance."

Wadsworth opens with a quote from Corinthians. "Know ye not your own selves."

"This question," he begins, standing very straight and tall and looking entirely at ease, "is exceedingly impressive as addressed to the Corinthians. They prided themselves in the Greek philosophy, and the very wisest of the precepts of that philosophy was—'Know thyself.'

"*We do not know our own selves!* A marvelous assertion, yet a true one. Physically, intellectually, morally, spiritually, most of men are to themselves profound strangers.

"Every man has his special intellectual gift, which often he does not discover till too late to develop and employ to profit."

Emily sits raptly, listening to his elegant discussion of the ways that men fool themselves. "Strange to say, few men understand rightly their own hypocrisies and disguises . . . The proud man looks after his covetousness—and the envious man looks after his dishonesty—and the impure man looks after his insincerity—each carefully perceiving, perhaps honestly confessing, some evil thing about him, which yet is not the elementary evil of his character. And thus reading himself wrongly, he manages himself also wrongly. He is busy cutting down thistles, and brambles, and thorns, while the oaks and cedars of iniquity shoot deep their strong roots, and spread wide their mighty branches."

As Emily sits in the far-off setting of Arch Street Church in Philadelphia, she understands something about the people of Amherst that has eluded her until now. Even basically good and decent people deceive themselves. They practice a kind of dishonesty of omission. It's what her friend Susan Gilbert sometimes does—willfully refusing to see the consequences of her actions—the way she draws people in, then shuts them out with the steel door of her disdain. Here in this church, Emily is being told something that she always knew, but wasn't aware that she knew.

She knows she must talk with this man.

TWO

The next morning, despite the cold mist and intermittent rain showers, Emily Dickinson makes the bold step of paying the Reverend Charles Wadsworth a visit in the study of his rectory, where he welcomes her with an air of polite forbearance.

He has no idea why she is there, and after some tentative, fumbling remarks about their mutual friends Lyman and Eliza Coleman, she cannot help but bring the subject around to poetry.

"I see that you have many books of poetry. Do you have any especial favorites?" She stands to read the titles.

He smiles. "That's difficult to say. I once fancied myself something of a poet," he tells her. "Before I realized the infirmities of the poetic impulse."

"Infirmities?" Emily asks, taking a seat again.

She suspects that he sees her as nothing but a nervous and eccentric young woman. She feels that her hair is too red, that she looks dowdy in her calico dress, that her face is too plain to please him, and that he will mistake her awkwardness for lack of intelligence. What she doesn't know is that he is already intrigued by her beautiful, dark, observant eyes, which have the openness of a child's and the directness of a cat's.

He walks around the desk and sits again facing her. "Don't you agree that so much of our poetry today is watery and vacuous and pure sentimental nonsense?"

"Oh, the foolish verses in the magazines, yes. But not the Brownings, surely."

"I hardly know them."

"But you know Tennyson." She glances up at the bookshelf.

"My wife gave me that volume. She's quite taken with him, and I've promised her that I will approach him with an open mind. But I have yet to feel his charms. I don't know—maybe my own poetry was so dreadful that it has made it impossible for me to appreciate anyone else's."

He shakes his head at his own poetic failings; she senses that he denigrates his efforts less out of modesty than out of some form of competition that he feels with his younger self.

"It is my feeling, Reverend Wadsworth, that you speak from the pulpit as a poet. Your sermon is poetry—the metaphors, the images, the feel for the sounds of words."

He laughs. "I don't admit to that at all." He touches a scar on his face.

"And why not?"

He looks at her so intensely that she feels he is seeing into her soul. "I take it that you are a poet?"

"I am not without hopes that I may be a poet, someday. I hope that someday I may make my family and friends proud of me."

"That's a noble sentiment. But to be a poet today, in our modern world in the middle of the nineteenth century . . . Miss Dickinson, would you mind if I quoted to you from one of my sermons?"

"I would be pleased."

Wadsworth stands up and strides over to a large wooden cabinet, which houses five or six drawers arranged vertically. He opens one of the drawers, rummages through it, and brings out a bundle of papers.

"This is from my Thanksgiving Day sermon of a few years ago. Here are my definitive thoughts on poetry. I wonder if they make any sense to you. Let's see, where to begin . . . Ah, here we are:

"'The poet, the creator of these later times, brings forth, not day dreams, but realities. The steam engine is a mightier epic than *Paradise Lost*. The magnetic telegraph is a lovelier and loftier creation of true poetry than Spenser's *Faery Queen* or Shakespeare's *The Tempest*.' And so on . . . Well, what do you think?"

"I am speechless."

He smiles at her with the glint in his eyes of an overgrown child who has confounded his elders. "Perhaps my interpretation of poetry is a bit too practical for your sensibilities?"

Her mouth makes a motion of dismay. "I find it bewildering and a bit sad, Reverend Wadsworth."

"How so?" He puts the sermon down and takes his seat again, crossing one leg over the other and leaning forward with an eager expression on his face.

"A modern machine is a wonderful thing. My own father formed a private company and brought the railroad to Amherst, and it is a marvelous creation—rather like a large cat that licks up miles instead of cream. But it is not a poem. Perhaps one day someone will write a poem about a railroad, but that's a different thing from the railroad's *being* a poem." She stops and looks at him.

"I'm not sure I quite follow you." A strange half-light is in his eyes. He rarely meets another person, man or woman, who can take him on successfully. He is beginning to realize that he has found her—or more accurately, that she has found him. And already he suspects—although it hardly seems possible—that she is more than his equal.

"Well, let's discuss the epic steam engine," Emily says, lingering with droll disingenuousness on the last three words. "No one would dispute that a steam engine is a magnificent and impressive machine. But it is *only* a machine. It can't be an epic because it has no meaning. Only function. *Paradise Lost* is an epic because it tells the story and the meaning of our fall from grace. A steam engine has no story to tell."

Wadsworth shakes his head. She has missed the point. He catches her eye and smiles knowingly, and he thinks he detects a flash of confusion or uncertainty on her face. The world is returning to its rightful orb. His arguments will prevail.

"But a steam engine is every bit as much a product of human imagination as *Paradise Lost*," he answers. "The poet here is a maker of things instead of a maker of words. Would you argue that poets may work only in words?"

She presses forward, undeterred.

"I fear that you are confusing the *products* of human imagination with those creations which themselves *embody* imagination. A broom is surely the product of intelligence—that's clear from its clever and useful design—and yet it has no intelligence itself. We who design and use the broom have the intelligence. And while a poem may not strictly be said to have intelligence—since it cannot speak or think—yet it does contain thoughts, images, words that work upon our minds with intellectual force."

He knows he has been painted into a corner. He smiles and shakes his head to buy a little time. He sees he has no recourse but to fall back on his wit.

"A broom may be said to work upon dirt with force," he observes.

She grants him a brief smile, but she is relentless.

"Then it may be admitted to contain the lowest form of intelligence, but nothing suited to the mind or spirit of man. Poems work in the higher spheres. An epic expresses the greatness of the spirit of one people or one race or the whole of humanity. A steam engine can only move a train, not hearts or minds."

He places his hands together before him—a preacherly gesture, a subtle effort to reclaim his position of masculine dominance. This is all mere words, his gesture seems to be saying. Stuff and nonsense.

"You are very persuasive," he tells her. "Yet you miss my point that the poetic imagination is seeking more practical avenues for its expression in this, our modern world." It is merely a defensive posture, and rather weak at that, he realizes, with more than a shred of annoyance.

She thinks of contradicting him but doesn't. She knows about proud men from her father, and she understands that this is his way of admitting defeat.

She responds not with an attack, but with an appeal to his prowess.

"I found your sermon yesterday in church exceedingly practical, because its spiritual thoughts taught me things about myself I never knew—or didn't know that I knew—in a way that a steam engine never shall. That is why I say you are a poet, Reverend Wadsworth—a far more mighty poet than the man who created the steam engine."

His masculine ego preens like a cat before a bowl of cream.

"You wrap your quarrel with me in the sweetest of compliments," he murmurs.

"I say nothing that I don't mean sincerely."

Those childlike eyes are fixed on him, with an expression he cannot read.

THREE

From the earliest moments of this, their first earthly meeting, Wadsworth has sensed that there is something different and unusual about his visitor. And, without his even realizing it, she has already made her way inside his first line of defenses. Now he looks at Emily with an air of fondness and familiarity that surprises him. As their conversation moves on to new topics—as she tells him about her recent trip with her father and sister to Washington, DC—he chuckles more than once at her remarks.

"Did you really find the pomp of Washington so difficult to bear?" he asks.

"It was nothing less than a capital offense," she replies, with an owlish glimmer in her eyes.

He blinks. "Are all the young ladies from Amherst as witty as you?" he asks, crossing one leg over another.

"I should hardly call myself 'witty'," she replies.

"I beg to differ. Tell me, during your trip to our

nation's capital with your esteemed father, did you treat the great men there to any of your witticisms?" he asks.

"Well, maybe once or twice." She looks down at her hands and folds them carefully.

"You make the most comical motions with your hands—has anyone ever told you that?" he asks.

"I find your directness rather disconcerting," she replies.

"Then I beg your pardon. But please do tell me at least one of your comments."

Emily sighs and placed her small hands on the arms of the chair, spreading out her fingers. She sees him watching her hands, and at once they both break out laughing.

"Forgive me," he says. "I find everything you do quite charming, and I mean no disrespect in any way."

"Well . . ." she begins, giving him a look, "One night we dined with a certain Supreme Court justice who was very starchy and proud of all the food that he served. For dessert they brought out a flaming pudding, and he was such a peacock about it that I couldn't resist an unfortunate comment."

"Don't hold back."

Emily extends her left hand before her and raises her right hand beside her head. "I said to him, 'Oh, Sir, may one eat of hell fire with impunity here?' To which he was speechless for a moment, and then he let go a great roar of laughter, stood up, tapped his glass, repeated the remark for all to hear, and claimed that it showed that the wit and sparkle of our young ladies from the provinces was a credit to our nation. And leaving me feeling as if I would like to crawl into my water glass."

Wadsworth lets go a great roar of laughter himself. "Well done, Miss Dickinson!" He shakes his head and laughs again. "But at this point the question arises: Did you meet any in Washington whom you did like?"

She falls into a strange silence. It takes her more than a few moments before she can find her words again, and she speaks haltingly, with the air of one who is making a solemn confession.

"Well, there was one man whom we adored. Thomas Dawes Eliot, Father's colleague in the House. He was not at all patronizing." A hint of humor crosses her face. "Or condescending. Or superior."

"I know the meaning of patronizing and condescending, thank you very much. What was it in particular about him that impressed you so?"

"You will probably laugh."

"Not at all."

"Well . . ." Emily says, a bit reluctantly, "he kissed his daughters goodnight each night before bed."

Wadsworth rests his hand against his cheek and frowns. He gives her a look, as if to determine if she is playing with him. She gazes toward him with an air of solemn sincerity.

"And why did that impress you so?" he asks finally.

"I told you that you would laugh."

"I'm not laughing. I'm just . . . a bit bewildered."

She folds her hands on her lap. She sits in rigid silence a moment. She sighs.

"Father has never done such a thing with us. In his entire life, he has never once kissed his daughters goodnight. Although he loves us in his way, as we know full well. Vinnie says he would die for us, but he would die first before letting anyone know it."

"I take it that Vinnie is your sister?" Although Wadsworth doesn't really understand what could be troubling Emily so, he knows it is time to change the subject.

"Yes, Vinnie is my younger sister."

"Oh, so there are two of you! Is she such a wit too?" He is smiling now: every inch the charming pastor wielding his masculine power to amuse, instruct, and put at ease a visitor and potential parishioner.

"I don't know. Some consider her more so, I suppose."

"And how do you consider her?" He places a finger to his lips; his brows crease slightly as if in serious thought, but the tone of his voice is light and playful.

Emily gazes off toward some distant realm where her life resides, and her voice grows slightly husky with the thought of home.

"She is totally necessary to my life. We may spend

a day without even talking, and yet I can't imagine life without her. It is as if we came up from two different wells, she is so different, yet life without her would be impossible."

He smiles and brings one hand up to his chin. "Would you mind if I ask, how is she different?"

"She is much more pert than I."

"Pert in spirit, or in body?"

"Both, but especially in body. Yet despite her pertness, she lives in a State of Regret, while I try to live in a State of Truth." She glances at him, with a tiny smile, apologizing for her grand pronouncement. His eyes catch hers, and a warmth passes between them.

"How interesting. It sounds to me as though your father has his hands full with the two of you. Is there another?"

"My brother Austin who is finishing his study of the law at Harvard and seems prepared to marry my good friend Susan Gilbert."

"Excellent! And a father who is a representative to Congress. Who I understand has proceeded back to Amherst to see your mother. But I have yet to hear any mention of your mother."

Again, Emily sits a moment in shivery silence. "My mother is an eternal mystery to us all."

"How so?"

Emily sighs. "She does all her household chores— sets a good table, sees to my father's effects and so forth—but she remains somehow distant and inscrutable. And in her own world."

"How unusual. Has she always been so?" He is thinking to himself, *the apple didn't fall far from the tree.*

"As long as I can remember. We always knew she loved us, and yet it was as though I had no mother growing up—in the sense of someone to whom children can go running with their day-to-day troubles. She was always so afraid for us, and for herself, and for her *luggage,* that we learned early to solve our problems ourselves or see them not solved at all."

"Her luggage?" he asks, smiling.

"Her luggage. Travel has ever been a great trial for my mother, for reasons none of us can fathom," she replies, with a force that discourages further questioning. He folds his hands under his chin and smiles. "I hope that our provincial ways do not seem laughable to you," she adds.

"On the contrary. Despite your semi-rustic origins, as far as I can tell, there is nothing of the backwoodsman life about you."

Those eyes turn to him with the directness that is still disturbing.

FOUR

Considering the moment, and choosing his words carefully, Wadsworth tips back his chair and purses his lips. "Now, how may I be of service to you?"

"I beg your pardon?" She looks up, startled. "How would I need any service?" Emily asks. "Not meaning to give any offense, of course."

He laughs, uncertainly. "None taken. It may be that it was I who was rude in offering you my services."

She realizes he is like her father in his dignity and at times in his sardonic humor, but he is altogether more fluid and supple and impossible to outflank.

"You were not rude," she replies. "I suppose when someone requests an audience with a minister, they do come seeking service of some sort or another."

"Very often," he agrees. "Though no promises are ever given. And in fact—for a minister—I make myself available much less than the average. I prefer my books, and my thoughts, and of course my family. I'm afraid I've gotten the reputation of being a recluse." He places one hand over the other and rubs it slightly, as if something on the hand pains him.

"But surely, a pastor cannot be a recluse for long," she observes.

He frowns. "If I allowed it, my entire day could be passed in a wearying succession of visits from busy-bodies who want to discuss order in the church, cranks who need to discuss God's providence, failed fellow pastors who wish me to obtain them a new situation . . . Churches—churches—sometimes I wish they were all burnt!"

"Heavens." She sits in silent alert, like a butterfly ready to flutter away.

He turns to her with a look of apology.

"Forgive me for alarming you. I'm nervous and tired today—tired mostly. I don't mean to lay my burdens upon you. Especially not when you have come out into such weather." The large window by his desk is beaded with raindrops.

"But I like the rain," she replies. "Do you hear how it makes two sounds at once?" She tilts her head in the direction of the window.

His brow wrinkles. She gestures toward the heavens.

"Listen. One sound is the close pitter patter of the large drops that roll off the roof onto the stones outside your window, and the other is the distant murmur where the rain strikes the high canopy of oak leaves."

He stands silent a moment. "I do hear them both. Very observant of you. I wonder—has the shower already brought out the robins?"

They go to the window. Three birds are hopping about on the lawn, plunging their beaks into the damp soil. "So it has!" he exclaims. "Look at them! Not a good day to be a worm."

"It rarely is," Emily replies.

He smiles. They both sit down again. She takes heart.

"I did wish to tell you one thing," she begins.

"And what was that?"

"When you spoke the other day . . . of those who refuse conversion because they have experienced no earth-shaking event or emotion . . ." She falls silent.

"Yes?" he prompts.

"You were describing me. You spoke directly to me." She looks down, ashamed.

"You are one who doubts, then."

"I doubt myself more than God, but yes, I doubt."

"I am one of those also, Miss Dickinson."

"But you can't be. You're a reverend."

He searches for her eyes, but can't find them.

"I have to think my way each week to salvation, because I never felt my way there. I am too full of doubts and tangled emotions. Each week is a struggle. Perhaps if I were more simple and trusting, I would not be such a recluse."

"How do you mean?" Emily asks, looking up at him and feeling that she can now return his directness.

"Because I can't offer a simple, pure faith—I can't come 'in white' to my congregation—then it follows that what I write and say in a sermon is more important than my pastoral relations with them." He shrugs.

"What does it mean to come 'in white'?" she asks.

"To appear before others in purity, in simplicity, in sincerity. Those are traits that I seem to possess only when I'm alone in my study."

Her dark eyes flash with understanding. "I also prefer to stay home and think. Many times I find myself inventing an excuse to stay home when Vinnie is buzzing off to her social engagements."

"But you don't stay home from church service, I hope?" he inquires with a slight smile.

"Sometimes I keep the Sabbath staying at home."

"In the garden, I hope?"

"Yes."

"God preaches there, I suppose."

"Exactly."

"And the sermon . . ." he asks.

"Is never long."

He smiles, simply and warmly.

"My dear Miss Dickinson, you are quite a puzzle. Every bit as much so as your mother."

FIVE

Charles Wadsworth is drawn to puzzles of all types—mathematical paradoxes, verbal conundrums, philosophical quibbles. And in the puzzle who sits facing him on this rainy March day, he detects a fellow traveler.

Already, a mesmerizing intimacy has begun to spread its web over them. Wadsworth turns to Emily, "Miss Dickinson, I detect true talent in you—talent of the rarest sort. People with a gift have an obligation to develop it to the fullest."

Her dark eyes pool with an expression he can't quite read—suspicion or defiance; her head begins to shake; she opens her mouth to speak.

He holds up a hand. "Please hear me out. I could get you enrolled in any graduate program in the East—at Princeton or Harvard—anywhere. With the greatest professors in the world. In philosophy, literature—even botany or biology if you prefer."

After a great effort, she almost manages a smile. "You are very kind, but I'm not interested."

"That seems curious."

"I tried once before, at Mount Holyoke, and it was not to my liking." Now her mouth has tightened into a grimace.

"But you enjoy learning?"

"Seminary was an impossible situation for all concerned."

Wadsworth frowns. "It's not often that I warn someone of their undeveloped gifts. I may never have occasion to do so again."

"Then I am grateful." There is no give in her countenance.

He tries to make a humorous and appealing face, but it goes against his grain and he looks at once silly and annoyed. He composes himself and says carefully, "I'm not going to give up on you. You have an assignment from me—to achieve greatness. By whatever means."

Now her dark eyes declare a new and different appeal, and to his surprise, they glimmer with what might be the onset of tears.

"Master, if you wish to assign greatness to me, I will do my best to complete my assignment," she says, folding her hands in her lap. For a moment she becomes still, as if sensing the stars wheeling on their invisible course somewhere above the city of Philadelphia.

"By writing poetry, I suppose," he growls, to hide his confusion and bewilderment.

"The steam engine has already been invented, so I feel I must return poetry to the realm of words." She glances at him. Both their moods have begun to alter like quicksilver. Now she is all impish humor, and he is falling into a cranky one.

"Very sardonic, Miss Dickinson."

She notes the look in his eyes. "I hope I am not the occasion of your bad mood."

"Not at all." Gloom sweeps over his face.

"Is there some way I can help you?"

"No, I am fine," he grumbles. He works his painful fingers.

"You are troubled."

Shivering, he says suddenly, "My life is full of dark secrets."

She sits without responding. He looks at her and smiles wanly. "Do I trouble you?"

"I could never think of any possible way that you could trouble me." She pauses a moment. "I don't know if I've expressed that strongly enough."

"You are kind to speak like that to an old, broken down man."

"You are neither old nor broken down."

He glowers. "When some men hear the mention of secrets, they blurt out immediately, 'Well, what are they?' Thank God you're not like that."

"Have no worry. A secret told ceases to be a secret then, so I would never ask."

"I wouldn't burden you with them, anyway."

"I have seen enough of life to know what a strain keeping things hidden can be." She sits quietly, staring straight ahead.

"Then it seems I am not the only one with particulars to hide."

Emily chooses not to answer. "I return to Amherst tomorrow, and I fear my Master will not remember me."

"Your fears are groundless. But I will not allow you to leave yet, if that is what you are threatening to do. It would be rude and unforgivable of me to receive you here without offering you some refreshment."

He steps out of the study and returns a few minutes later with a woman, considerably younger than he, carrying a tray on which are set slices of bread, a jar of jam, a pot of butter, and some knives.

"Emily Dickinson, I have the pleasure of introducing you to my wife, Jane Locke Wadsworth."

"So pleased to meet you," Emily says.

"The pleasure is mine," Jane answers. "Charles was telling me about you and your family. I understand Lyman is your cousin." She sets down the tray and approaches Emily, smiling. In the custom of the day, they kiss on the cheek. She looks at Emily with curiosity in her large, intelligent gray eyes. Her raven hair is parted in the middle and falls in ringlets to her shoulders. Her face is serious and pious—more righteous somehow than her husband's. Emily senses that she is someone who observes closely and makes private judgments that she hides behind an habitual air of friendliness.

"Would you like butter or jam on your bread?" Jane asks.

"Just a touch of butter, please," Emily replies. "I hate to obscure the simple sincerity of graham bread with anything so boisterous as jam."

Jane smiles and butters a slice, which she places on a plate and brings over to the guest. "Pray have a seat while you eat. I take it that you bake your own version— perhaps a New England recipe that is unknown to us?"

"I'm sure it's very similar—all the versions must trace their lineage directly back to Dr. Graham and his theories of healthy eating."

Wadsworth clears his throat. "A bit of a crank, Graham. A minister who never preached a day in his life. If he had his way, none of us would eat animal products, and as for the side effects on families and progeny . . ." He falls silent at a quick, stern glance from his wife.

Emily picks up the slice and bites into it delicately. "Oh, this is very good. And it's so much better eaten like this—still warm."

"It's because of the heaviness of the crushed kernel," Jane replies.

"I think that must be it. If you allow it to grow cold, it recalls its earthly weight—but warm, it still ascends to the skies. This is divine."

"If you don't mind my asking, how much lard do you use in yours?" Jane asks.

"About half a gill."

"Is that all? I often use close to one full gill."

"That must be why this is moist and luscious. Perhaps I'll experiment when I get home," Emily says. It is difficult for her to eat her portion—knowing the amount of lard has made it unbearably heavy and dull—but she presses on.

"Are you the bread-maker in the family?" Jane asks, looking at her with an air of sympathy that barely conceals a too-intense inquiry.

"Father insists on it. He says he will have my bread or none at all."

"What will he do should you ever marry, I wonder?" Jane asks smiling.

"I shall have to make a double batch each morning and send one of them over to him with my husband. Father simply wouldn't abide anything else."

"How interesting the families in New England are. The old, close ties are still very strong."

"It's the cold winters, no doubt about it," Wadsworth puts in. He has been standing off to the side, watching with pleasure as the two women talk.

"The cold winters, Charles?" his wife asks him, rolling her eyes ever so slightly toward him.

He proceeds to explain a theory he has developed: Opposites always adhere. Cold and adversity have the effect of drawing forth warmth and strong bonds among family members. It's the law of life, he says. All growing things depend for their progress on constant antagonisms.

"Not all frictions are to be wished for, though," Jane remarks.

"That's true. But neither can they all be avoided. And many of them, paradoxically, purify the organism and lead it to a condition of higher excellence. Although, if that were always the case, I should be more excellent than I am," he finishes with a smile and a shrug. Emily sees that he is accustomed to behaving better—and to concealing his gloom—when in the presence of his wife.

"Now, dear, we know you're an excellent man in all ways," Jane teases him.

"I agree with your law of antagonism," Emily says. She is aware that Jane Wadsworth is watching her very carefully.

"How do you mean?" Wadsworth asks.

"Well, take the acorn," she replies. She describes something she has just read in one of Professor Hitchcock's books—the famous professor of geology who had recently stepped down as president of Amherst. When an acorn falls to the ground, destructive agents in the soil immediately try to destroy it. But what they actually do is weaken the husk so that the germ can grow. "Before you know it, a green blade has worked its way out of the earth and is seeking sunlight and freedom," she concludes.

"Miss Dickinson, you speak beautifully, and you have the most remarkable eyes," Jane Wadsworth tells her.

"Oh no, it's you who has the beautiful eyes," Emily replies. "They are the color of twilight. A most witching color." She falls silent, thinking perhaps she has spoken too boldly.

"Thank you. And your eyes are like the finest amber. Though darker," Jane answers.

"I always tell people my eyes are the color of the sherry which the guest leaves in the glass."

"Another wonderful image," Wadsworth remarks. "I wish you lived closer to Philadelphia, Miss Dickinson, because I have no doubt that you two would quickly become fast friends."

"Have you lived in Philadelphia long?" Emily inquires.

Jane Wadsworth replies that they have lived in the city for five years. They met when Wadsworth was a pastor in Troy, New York—she fell in love with him while a girl in seminary, hearing him preach. They spent their first several years of married life in Troy.

"It's very romantic, a new husband and wife making such a move," Emily offers.

"It was," Jane acknowledges.

"I suppose you have a young family which takes much of your time and care?" Emily asks Jane.

"No—not yet," Jane replies. Behind her twilight eyes, Emily senses the stirring of darker shades. "Perhaps some day."

"We feel in no rush to establish a family," her husband adds. He is standing behind his cane chair, and he starts to tap a finger on its curved wooden top.

"Of course," Emily agrees. "It's always best to wait a few years, although children must be a dear addition to any family."

A fleeting expression crosses Wadsworth's face, like the ghost of some remembered slight or pain.

"Would you care for another slice of bread, Miss Dickinson?" Jane asks.

Emily politely declines.

"Then in that case, I think I will withdraw. I have some housework which awaits me."

Emily stands. "It was nice to meet you, and partake of your lovely sustenance, which makes me feel suddenly quite homesick."

"The pleasure was all mine." Jane picks up the tray.

"Let me help you with that," her husband says.

"I do not need any help, my dear husband." She glides out of the room with the tray.

"You have a charming and lovely wife," Emily says. Even to a minister, she reflects, Mrs. Wadsworth's rectitude must be daunting.

"All who know her admit her excellence," he remarks, "but I alone know and appreciate the full extent of it." He has returned to his desk, and he shuffles through a few papers. Emily senses that this might be a signal for her to take her leave.

"Reverend Wadsworth?" Emily asks.

"Yes?" He seems awakened from a troublesome reverie.

"I thought your wife was quite lovely."

"Thank you."

"But I had a question."

"You may ask."

Emily takes a deep breath. "When the subject of family came up, I felt that she pulled in her head and arms and closed the shell. Or perhaps that she spread her wings and fluttered away."

"You may have felt that."

"Did you feel that?"

Now the darker shades stir behind his eyes.

"I love my wife dearly, and all the more so because of what I know, and what no other mortal suspects."

"Then I will ask no more."

"You have an alarming way of not asking about secrets and at the same time asking about them, Miss Dickinson."

"I am sorry."

Wadsworth gives her a penetrating look. "You still refuse my offer of assistance with your higher education?"

"I do."

"How then shall I know when you have attained greatness?"

"I will send you flowers."

He smiles. "That's charming."

"If I am great, they will speak to you."

As they parted, did either of them—the poet and the pastor—realize how loudly these flowers would one day speak?

SIX

Summer, 1855

When Emily Dickinson returned to Amherst, the surface of her life continued as it always had, unblemished.

She rose before dawn, started the bread, took Carlo for a walk and set the dough to rise. She observed the birds, the sky, the slant of light against a wall, then jotted down a line or two of verse.

But she no longer felt complete in her stillness; in fact, she felt strangely troubled.

Beneath the surface, her life was altering. Though Emily Dickinson and Charles Wadsworth would remain physically apart for the next five years—between 1855 and 1860—the axes of their two worlds had begun to tilt toward each other.

How—during those five years apart—did the sparks set flying by their intense, sometimes contentious discussions in Philadelphia kindle into the full

blaze of obsessive passion? Certainly Emily knew
even then that their meeting was a transcendent moment—but what she felt was not love and certainly not
sexual passion. Rather, it was the breathless adulation
that talented students feel for a respected teacher who
recognizes their gifts. And for his part, though Charles
Wadsworth was more savvy than Emily about the possible ramifications—after all, his own wife had first
fallen in love with him by listening to him preach—he
was puzzled, amused and annoyed by Emily's prickli-
ness and did not find her attractive physically. He was
also happily married. What happened?

We have all seen it happen before—say, two col-
leagues who work together and are the best of friends.
Each of them cozily married with stable, successful
families. No hint of romantic or sexual attraction between them. Then one spring, he develops a painful
condition—let's say a frozen shoulder. As part of his
therapy he needs someone to help him extend his arm
in different directions.

Twice a day, for about ten minutes at a time, openly and in the presence of others, she moves his arm in
various directions that hurt him terribly. They talk only
minimally as they work. "Is that the right direction?"
"Yes, go higher." The interaction is mostly silent. But
in that silence, in that physical contact that defines the
boundaries of pleasure and pain between them, they
fall deeply in love. Somehow they reach the kindling

point, and all the fuel of friendship leaps gloriously and horribly into flame. Within a year they divorce their spouses and are living together. Ten years later, they are still together, the happiest couple anyone knows. The children and former spouses are still recovering. All because of a touch.

What was the touch between Emily Dickinson and Charles Wadsworth in those five years apart?

It was their letters.

۶۶

The act of writing each other was hazardous. Though a young woman might correspond with a married minister now and then, any frequent contact would be sure to cause a murmur in town. The post-master knew exactly who was writing to whom, and often knew why. He was not known for his discretion. The last thing Emily wanted was a whiff of scandal. For his part, any hint of adultery could have ended Wadsworth's extraordinary career in the pulpit.

Early on, Emily and Wadsworth established a cover. She enclosed her letters to Wadsworth in correspondence that she sent to a longtime family friend, Mrs. J. G. Holland of Springfield, Massachusetts. Mrs. Holland then forwarded the letters to Wadsworth, who wrote back to Mrs. Holland as the go-between. That way the Amherst postmaster never saw a letter addressed in her hand to the famous minister.

Those letters they wrote one another, across the hundreds of miles between Amherst and Philadelphia, allowed them to stretch each other's arms, extend each other's reach, and touch somehow a shared boundary of pleasure and pain.

SEVEN

Fall, 1855

That November the family made its long-anticipated return to the Dickinson Homestead on Main Street. Emily's grandfather had disgraced the family by losing the house to creditors fifteen years earlier, and in 1854 Edward finally repurchased it and spent a year renovating and improving the mansion for the family's triumphant return.

But the move was harder on everyone than expected—and the house was strangely forbidding, a massive, three-story brick building in the Federal style, painted a dull mustard. It was symmetrical except for its left wing, on the front of which a glass conservatory had been added so that Emily could keep plants year-round. An imposing entryway, complete with Ionic columns, greeted the visitor. A newly constructed wooden cupola looked down on all of Amherst. The house faced south and overlooked its broad eleven-acre meadow, a hat factory, the Connecticut River valley, and the distant charcoal smudge of Mount Holyoke. The windows were large and shuttered. The building was situated up the hill from the road and could be reached by climbing a succession of humbling, broad stone steps. It spoke of power and grandeur rather than beauty.

It wasn't just the move itself that was difficult—Mother's health had become a serious concern. No one knew what ailed her. It might have been an allergy to something in the house (perhaps the new paint) or it might have been unhappiness at leaving their happy home on West Street and returning to the site of their stressful early years as a family. It might have been a back problem or something to do with nerves. Vinnie and Emily attended to her all day in the back parlor.

"Mother," Emily calls. "I've brought you some eggs this morning. Newly laid, and nicely poached, just as you like them. And some Indian and rye bread, of course."

Mother doesn't answer.

"It's a beautiful day—mild and sunny for January. I do believe the birds will be singing later," Emily informs her.

Mother doesn't answer.

Emily pulls in a little table and sets the food on it

for her—eggs, bread, a glass of milk with beady bubbles at the edges.

"Mother, you must eat, dear."

Again, Mother doesn't answer. Her eyes are dim and ungiving. She is looking at everything and nothing. Her hands clasp the arms of her easy chair. Her back and neck are rigid, and her shoulders feel like steel.

"Just one bite, darling," Emily says. She lifts a spoonful of egg to her mother's lips. The white and yellow goo drips from her lips and dribbles down her chin. Emily dabs it off with a napkin and tries again. "Come on, darling. One more time. Let's get some food into the body. How are we to worship the Lord without a little fuel for the fire?" She tries again, with no more success.

Setting down the bowl and spoon she kneels beside her mother. "Is there anything we can do to help, Mother? Is there anything at all you would like? We just don't know what to do, dearest." She smoothes back her mother's salt-and-pepper hair.

Vinnie appears in the doorway. "Any success?"

"She is the Sphinx."

"Wiser probably than the rest of us, who say so much yet so little."

Emily stands up and throws her hands over her head. "It's your turn, Vinnie. I just don't know what to do." She glances out the window, and her tone of voice becomes deliberately casual. "By the way, do you know if we received yesterday's post?"

"No, it was delayed. Are you expecting something?"

"Oh, nothing particular."

"I notice you've been writing often to the Hollands."

"Oh yes, they are wonderful and understanding people—don't you think? Mrs. Holland is a dear."

"Well, yes, I suppose." They give each other a passing glance as Vinnie comes over to sit by Mother. "Now Mother, that's enough pretending. Let's do some eating and some talking, and then you can snooze if you like. This Sphinx act is not helping you or anyone else, dear."

Emily goes upstairs. She closes the door and looks through the growing pile of letters. Over the next few years they will slowly, inexorably fill an entire box that she keeps carefully hidden in her dresser.

EIGHT

1856 – 1859

Austin and Emily's childhood friend, Susan Gilbert, were married in Geneva, New York on July 1, 1856. Soon afterwards, the couple moved into the chic new Italianate villa next door that Father built for them. Given the name "The Evergreens," it was a stunning, exquisite house unlike anything else in Amherst— asymmetrical, with a flat roof and a high central tower, tall elegant windows, and a wide veranda.

Every detail was perfect: the evergreen hedges and landscaping by Frederick Law Olmsted, the stone-colored siding and green shutters to match the natural setting, the beautiful arched front doors, the built-in bookcases in the parlor, the new and useful feature known as a hall closet, the button in the floor of the dining room by Susan's place at the table so she could summon the servants without disturbing the dinner guests.

Set back from the road and approached by a sweeping walkway, its beauty and grace offered visitors an implicit promise of a lovely new world.

Susan became a brilliant hostess who spent hours in the kitchen supervising servants and doing the preparation herself for the "star" dishes. A typical menu for a dinner party featured a starting course of borscht, followed by roast oysters with truffles, poached salmon, roast of lamb with new potatoes and spring vegetables, and a chocolate gelato for dessert—all served with appropriate wine, sherry, port and after-dinner liquors. When she wasn't attending the dinner herself, Emily often sent over a loaf of bread or a flower, accompanied by an enigmatic little note or poem.

I send a Violet, for Libby. I should have sent a stem, but was overtaken by snow drifts. I regret deeply, not to add a Butterfly.

🍀

Through 1859 and most of 1860, Emily was taking an active part in the social whirlwind next door.

The library, or parlor as it was also called, was a center of activity. It was a warm, comfortable, but refined room furnished with splendid sofas and chairs, a grand piano, and several large, striking oil paintings. Although Austin favored a bold landscape from Norway, the few works from the Hudson River School were the true prizes of his growing art collection. They hung on the wall to the right of the entrance. Just inside the doorway was the open area where Susan stood when she read poetry aloud—often an affectionate little verse from her sister-in-law.

Also to the right, back in the corner stood the piano that Emily sometimes played after dinner for the guests. She could bring the after-dinner pleasantries to a meditative hush with the eerie, fractured melodies that she composed herself. She could stir the guests to rowdy songfest with her sophisticated arrangements of popular songs such as "Auld Lang Syne" and "Believe Me If All Those Endearing Young Charms"; and she could astonish the listeners with her flawless renditions of the virtuoso classical pieces of the time such as "Sliding Waltz."

In the far corner of the room was the large chair where Ralph Waldo Emerson sat when he visited the Evergreens.

Ambitious, high-minded, witty, charming, Susan Dickinson was never so alive as when she hosted a dinner party. Through gesture, tone of voice, and intuitive reading of people and situations, she completely dominated the room. Guests felt important and appreciated in her presence; she drew from their fame and sense of accomplishment and gave their heightened self-worth back to them enriched with her clever, informed comments.

"More oysters?" she inquires of the newspaper editor in her most melodious tone. "We cannot let Samuel Bowles walk away from the table without his fill of oysters."

"No thank you, Susan dearest," the young man replies. His dark hair and beard gleam handsomely. "Any more and I shall burst." He turns back to Austin.

"Might I ask what you and Austin are so busily engaged in discussing?" Susan asks, with a teasing lilt in her voice.

"Oh, the usual. The new painting by Gignoux, and how we both wish we could afford it," Samuel replies, as Austin looks toward her impassively.

"Well, I'm sure great men like you are entitled to whatever they want," Susan purrs, and turns to speak to another guest.

Emily is perched on her chair like a bird, glancing about and taking it all in. In the midst of the eating, the drinking, the good-natured banter, she begins to recall the room's history, how it was constructed from the shabby rental cottage that occupied the space before the Evergreens was built. Now, with its exquisite paneled wood ceiling, and its dark blue, textured wallpaper in the William Morris style, the room reveals no sign of its humble past. As Vinnie likes to point out, Susan began in equally humble ways—as the daughter of an innkeeper—and she now puts on impossibly fancy airs.

NINE

In the fall of 1858 with Mother showing no improvement, Father takes her off to Northampton for a water cure, and Emily's old friend Eliza Coleman pays a visit.

"And how have you been, my darling?" Eliza asks Emily. She takes off her bonnet and shakes out her blond hair. She has put on a fair amount of weight, and by the styles of the time she is plump and pretty and highly desirable.

"Oh, it's been hectic around here." Emily fills her in on the news about Austin and Susie.

"It must be exciting to have them both so close," Eliza says.

"Just a hedge away."

"And is Susie behaving herself?"

"Susan fronts on the Gulf Stream."

"Well put. Changeable and tempestuous."

Emily looks at Eliza and pauses a moment.

"Eliza, did you know I've been corresponding with the Reverend Wadsworth?" she asks.

"No, I didn't. How very nice!"

"Yes. It is."

Emily tells Eliza about the written conversations she and the Reverend Wadsworth have been conducting on a myriad of topics: the nature of poetry, the importance of attending a church service each Sunday, the wisdom of keeping a dog as a pet.

"I tried to convince him that a dog has a soul every bit as deep and refined as a human's, and he laughed it off entirely . . . if a letter can be said to laugh. But letters such as his seem to have the sentience of a living thing. They possess the full range of human feeling and speculation."

Eliza frowns at her friend's ardor, which grows all the more apparent the more Emily talks.

By the end of the conversation Eliza is looking off across the valley towards Mount Holyoke, and though she says nothing, she cannot quite hide her air of disquiet.

"Do you know what's so strange and wonderful, Eliza?" Emily asks.

"No," Eliza replies.

"How gentle he is. He is my dearest Earthly friend."

"Charles Wadsworth is a fine and even majestic man, and a true friend of my father," Eliza says carefully, but her eyes glitter uneasily.

By late 1858 Mother is finally well again. Her recovery

is as mysterious as her illness. She is moving about and talking and seems indisposed to discuss whatever it was that has immobilized her for almost two years.

Now that Emily doesn't need to tend to Mother as much, she is free to turn even more of her attention to the remarkable letters that Charles Wadsworth is sending her—warm, supportive, funny, confiding. By now the box hidden inside her dresser is almost half full. Late at night, when it is finally safe for her to take out the letters and feast her eyes on them, she removes the envelopes one at a time, holding them in her small deft hands as reverently as if they were butterfly wings. She lovingly pulls an envelope apart at the cut in the top and painstakingly draws forth the creamy paper with the Arch Street Presbyterian Church heading. She unfolds it, sits cross-legged on her bed by the lamp, and reads again his closely reasoned, elegant expressions of his many interests—including, not least of all, his interest in her. He has not declared his love for her, but she can feel it in every word he writes.

She thinks of him with each waking breath. He is the standard against which she measures the world and the unseen arbiter of her daily disappointments and aspirations. Though she hasn't seen him in three years, the world is drenched with his presence. He is as real and unchanging as the sun hidden only for now by a passing cloud. And the force of that sun quickens the lines of her poetry with new brilliance and light.

TEN

At the floodtide of this new love in 1858, still amazed at the depth of what she feels and full of hope that cannot even begin to anticipate fear or disappointment, she writes to the Reverend. Her wistful sentences flow with tender concern for his health and radiate a gentle, almost elegiac appreciation of a world made beautiful by her love.

Dear Master

I am ill, but grieving more that you are ill, I make my stronger hand work long eno' to tell you. I thought perhaps you were in Heaven, and when you spoke again, it seemed quite sweet, and wonderful, and surprised me so – I wish that you were well.

I would that all I love, should be weak no more. The Violets are by my side, the Robin very near, and "Spring" – they say, Who is she – going by the door –

Indeed it is God's house – and these are gates of Heaven,

*and to and fro, the angels go, with their sweet postillions – I
wish that I were great, like Mr. Michael Angelo, and could
paint for you. You ask me what my flowers said – then they
were disobedient – I gave them messages. They said what the
lips in the West, say, when the sun goes down, and so says
the Dawn.*

*Listen again, Master. I did not tell you that today had
been the Sabbath Day.*

*Each Sabbath on the Sea, makes me count the Sabbaths,
till we meet on shore – and whether the hills will look as blue
as the sailors say. I cannot talk any more tonight, for this
pain denies me.*

*How strong when weak to recollect, and easy, quite, to
love. Will you tell me, please to tell me, soon as you are well.*

And the man who reads this extraordinary statement of love—the man who apparently didn't understand the poems (flowers) that she has been enclosing
in her letters to him since 1855?

For years Wadsworth has loved his wife in a clas-
sic, nineteenth-century way—a mix of thankfulness,
proprietary interest, tenderness, shared hope for their
children's future, and arrogance. He has more than
admired the way Jane has accepted her affliction in
silence. She has made it through the tough years, the
years of miscarriages when the disease that he passed
on to her was still active—that period of time before it
entered its latent stage and allowed healthy children to

be born. This difficulty is something they both know, yet never mention. All is well now. She occupies a comfortable, unassailable spot in his affections. At first Emily was but a drip of water making a slight stain through those feelings—a discomfort, almost like the memory of something unpleasant. But the letters have kept flowing, full of startlingly original thoughts that intrigue him, appeals to his affection that somehow charm him, expressions of devotion to his wisdom that flatter him, heretical musings on religion that strike a chord in him; and slowly, over time, those drips of water have opened up a new cavern, secret and wild, where his feelings for her can take residence, be nourished and grow.

These feelings in the Reverend are new and unsuspected. How better to win the love of a happily married man, than by making him new to himself? And so it is—though he may feel it is nothing more than pastoral concern for one of the straying daughters of the church—in truth he is hers. And she—too caught up in the strength of her feelings for him, in the fact of her love, to suspect that she has already won him—she has no idea that she must claim him at their next meeting, or never at all.

Part II

Again – his voice is at the door –
I feel the old Degree –
I hear him ask the servant
For such an one – as me . . .

ELEVEN

Summer, 1860

For a week Emily has known Wadsworth is coming. She knows he is staying with his friend Charles Clark at the Clark summer house in Northampton that June, and she knows he has been waiting for the weather to clear before he visits her. For a week she has hardly slept, suspended between ecstasy and despair.

❧

"I am here to call on Miss Dickinson." *His voice at the door.*

The long-imagined words rupture the membrane between heaven and earth. Here, at her home, his voice sounds deeper and grainier than she remembers and somehow more dangerous—almost illicit. She pictures him standing just outside the front door, holding his hat in his hands, perhaps glancing over his shoulder and admiring the view of the Connecticut River valley stretching off to the south towards Mount Holyoke. In the moment that she creates this mental picture, his physical presence becomes strikingly real to her; as she hears him speak again, it becomes frightening and altogether dear.

"Which Miss Dickinson, if you don't mind, sir?" Margaret asks.

"Miss Emily Dickinson."

She is in the back parlor reading her favorite novelist, George Eliot. Mother and Father have gone for the day to visit relatives in Springfield. Vinnie has strolled into town to shop. It is just Emily and Margaret, the serving girl. Despite being called the girl, Margaret is a formidable woman, in personality as well as girth. A year or two older than Emily, she weighs twelve stone and can wield a cleaver like a butcher.

"May I tell her who's calling, if you please?"

"The Reverend Charles Wadsworth."

He has pronounced his name, his blessed name, there on the very portal of Emily's home. Already Emily feels the rush of wings as heaven descends onto Earth.

Heavy footsteps in the hall. Margaret's voice. "Miss Dickinson, there is a visitor."

"Yes, Margaret, I know."

"It's a gentleman, miss." She stands there before Emily, colossal and slow.

"I know that too, Margaret."

"Do you think I should let him in?" Margaret gazes

toward her with dull cunning. "It's a gentleman, miss." Her body has the proportions of a child, with her round belly and short legs, but she is easily three times the size of a child.

"Of course you should let him in. He is a reverend, Margaret."

"So he said."

"Did you doubt his word?"

"He's wearing mourning in his hat." Her look of cunning intensifies, her upper lip curls suspiciously.

"Well, ministers mourn too sometimes. Let him in, for God's sake."

"Yes, miss."

More heavy footsteps. A small, wary voice. "You may come in, sir."

"Thank you. Miss Dickinson is not indisposed?"

"No sir."

Emily walks—no floats—into the front parlor. On the way she plucks a daisy from a vase. She can see a man in the front hall. He dwarfs the colossal Margaret. He is much larger than Emily remembers, with big shoulders and a massive head. A bison has entered her father's house.

He turns and sees her. He is not smiling, but humor plays over his face like far-off sheet lightning.

"Reverend Wadsworth," she croaks.

"Miss Dickinson," he replies in his low voice. "What a pleasure to see you again."

"There are no words that express my delight. Ecstasy is only a shadow to what I feel." She moves forward and stops a few feet from him, tottering in amazement at his imminence. "Here," she says, thrusting the flower toward him. "A daisy follows the sun." She looks up at him, then away as if her eyes cannot stand the brilliance.

He takes the flower graciously and stands admiring it. He is easily twenty or thirty feet tall.

They have not even shaken hands.

She can feel Margaret watching the scene in amazement. Emily has received no male callers for several years; almost all of her socializing took place at the Evergreens, her brother Austin's house next door. At the age of twenty-nine, she is assumed to have no male admirers. And here is this reverend, clearly a man of importance, quite possibly married, addressing Emily in the most familiar of terms. Margaret's mouth has actually fallen open, and she has become something gargantuan frozen in stone, a petrified gargoyle.

"Margaret?"

No response.

"Margaret?"

"Yes, Miss Dickinson?"

"There is some graham bread in the oven."

"Yes, Miss Dickinson." Margaret eyes Emily suspiciously; her mouth puckers with doubt and misgiving.

"Will you kindly take it out?"

"Are you sure it's ready, miss?"

"Well, even if it's not, take it out anyway."

"No, Miss Dickinson."

"I'm joking, Margaret."

"Yes, Miss Dickinson."

"You may go, Margaret."

"Yes, Miss Dickinson." Slowly, like someone maintaining eye contact with a wild animal so it won't charge, Margaret backs out of the room.

Once she is gone, Wadsworth purses his lips and shakes his head. "Is she always so amusing?" he asks.

"I should think not. Poor dear, I don't know if she will ever walk forward again."

"I take it my visit comes as something of a shock?"

"From Margaret's point of view, your presence here is no less remarkable than if I were to receive a visit from Moses. Complete with the burning bush and the tablet of the Ten Commandments."

"Your parents are not in?"

"They are visiting family in Springfield. I hope you had a nice ride here."

"Very nice. Delightful, in fact. Your country—these hills—truly are the gates of heaven. At least so they seem to a visitor from the South."

She notices a painful-looking red swelling on the back of one of his hands. Other than that, he looks in excellent health—no sign of stiffness or difficulty in moving.

"How long was your ride?"

"About an hour."

"How did you come?"

"By carriage, of course."

"I meant the route you followed."

He tries to describe his route, but her face remains blank. She gazes at him with a fixed, uncomprehending expression, as though he were talking in some strange language. So he starts again, this time enunciating his words like a country schoolmaster, highlighting the important phrases with cheery, labored pedantry.

"Well, I started up the *Connecticut River valley*"—he takes a few steps forward towards the stairs by way of illustration—"and then cut across on the road that follows the *creek to Hadley*"—he turns at a sharp angle to the right of the stairs—"and proceeded past Hadley until I connected with the *Amherst road*"—he turns left again, takes a few more strides, and comes to a stop partway down the hall. He turns toward her, fully aware of the ludicrous contrast between his dark clothes, his prancing steps, and his lugubrious delivery.

"What a curious way to chart a map," she remarks, following the path of his footsteps with her own small steps, throwing her hands up in the air as she pivots so quickly on the turning points that she feels a catch in her knee.

"I'm doing nothing that you didn't discuss at some length in Philadelphia."

Emily floats up to him and stops. She knows she is closer than she should be, but she does not back away. She is near enough to place her head on his shoulder if she dared. "Reverend Wadsworth, I don't recall saying anything about reducing someone else to a fool by talking down to them," she says. Her breathless, childlike voice plays seductively upon his ears.

His face registers pain. "You certainly didn't, and I beg your pardon. I was only trying to be amusing. But it's clear I failed."

"Then consider me amused, for I'm sure I shall be in the weeks ahead as I look back on your amazing performance. But I am interested in hearing what you think I said in Philadelphia."

His eyes look into hers, near and far away at the same time. "You spoke long and eloquently about metaphor, and the way that one thing becomes something else yet remains itself. That is the work of a poet, you said. Well, your hall is now a metaphor, and by walking—not by talking—I am now a poet." He looks toward her with his inscrutable roguery.

"You were a poet with words long before you took your bold steps down this hall in the house of my father," she says with a tender, almost sorrowful tone in her voice. She suddenly feels the weight of his visit and wonders if she will be able to bear it.

His voice is gentle. "And yet it is wonderful that a hall can be a representation of a region. And that we can look at one and see the other. And that we can look upon each other."

"From this day forward this hallway shall be known as the Charles Wadsworth projection of the Connecticut River valley, Northampton to Amherst," she says. And she thinks: *For five years I have been looking at his letters and seeing him, but now that he is here, I feel I* don't *see him, and I can't possibly say what I want to say.*

He seems to read her thoughts. "I've been looking forward to this day," he says. "You left such an impression on me, though it was five years ago. And your wonderful letters . . ." He seems unable to continue.

For over five minutes now, Emily Dickinson has been welcoming Charles Wadsworth into her father's home in Amherst, and she is stunned at the familiarity yet strangeness of it all.

"I take it that your rheumatism is behaving?" she asks Wadsworth, as he shifts from foot to foot in the front hallway.

"It is much better, thank you."

He is turning his hat in his hand, and she sees he is wearing black in his hat. "Someone has died?"

"Yes. My mother."

"Did you love her?"

"Yes," he replies in his deep voice.

"I am sorry."

"That I loved her?" The humor plays over his face, far away, a ghostly flicker.

"That you lost her."

"She was very good to me. Even when she knew the worst."

"There were no secrets from your mother?"

"There are never secrets from a mother."

Margaret appears in the hallway behind Wadsworth.

"Yes, Margaret?" Emily asks.

"Pardon miss, but will the gentleman be staying to dine?"

"No, Margaret. We are going for a walk."

A glimmer stirs deep in Margaret's small, unblinking eyes. "A walk, miss?"

"Yes."

"By yourselves, miss?"

"No."

"No, miss?"

"Not by ourselves. With Carlo."

Again, Margaret's mouth falls open.

"Reverend Wadsworth, do you feel it would be precipitous were I to introduce you to Carlo at this time?"

"Not at all," he replies. Taking his hand for a second, she leads him down the back hall, around the frozen effigy of Margaret, past the "Northwest passage" (a doorway to the back stairs where Emily and Austin sometimes meet in private), and through the kitchen to the back door. There, luxuriating in his little home, is Carlo.

The memory of the quick touch of Wadsworth's hand is still in Emily's palm and in her mind and in her heart—the gentle, strong contact that says, *I know why I am here but I can't say it aloud.*

Carlo groans and pulls himself up—head and front feet first, then his massive backside. He takes a few polite steps out of his house, snorts a few times, looks up at Emily and wags his tail with a questioning, faintly hopeful air.

He sniffs at her hand with his black, dimpled nose to see if she has brought him a treat. He studies her again with large brown eyes that seek a motive.

"Carlo, this is Reverend Wadsworth."

As if he understands, the dog shambles over to Wadsworth, his sides heaving from side to side like a boat rolling in rough swells. He gets a whiff of the minister's hands and allows his head to be scratched.

"Delighted and honored to meet you, Carlo," Wadsworth announces.

The dog gazes at him and snorts. He shakes his head, and his ears flop loudly.

"Amazing. He sounds exactly like a pigeon taking off," Wadsworth comments.

Carlo sneezes and looks at Wadsworth.

"He wants you to scratch his head again," Emily tells him.

"He does, does he?"

Carlo butts his head against Wadsworth's hip.

"I think you'd better scratch him very soon. He likes you."

"And if I don't, does he like me so much that he might knock me down?"

"Quite possibly."

Wadsworth scratches the dog between his ears. Carlo tilts his head back, closing his eyes against the pleasure.

"Carlo has a theory of ultimate pleasure," Emily explains.

"How so?" Still scratching.

"Whenever he is given an especially nice bone from dinner, he looks for the most comfortable spot possible where he can lie and enjoy it. Once he slipped into the house with a juicy bone and found Father's best easy chair in the parlor. Father was not amused."

"I should think not."

"Carlo is my good friend. He is always quiet and exhibits great tact."

"You have the most comical servant and the most waggish dog I've ever seen," Wadsworth observes. He has stopped scratching, and Carlo is breathing heavily and scrutinizing him. The dog has begun to pant, and the tip of his pink tongue protrudes beyond his teeth.

"It seems you find everything about me amusing."

"You know that's not true," he tells her, patting the dog's head one last time. There is a pause. Somewhere in the distance a crowd of blue jays scolds a cat.

"You see my little garden," Emily says, nodding toward the side yard. Roses luxuriate in the full bloom of the midday sun.

"I would not call it little." Wadsworth has been observing Emily's eyes. They are an unusual reddish brown, like a liquor, or perhaps like one of the new plastic compounds that a parishioner of his, a chemical engineer, has been developing for all sorts of everyday uses—everything from billiard balls to false teeth. There is a density about them—not of color, but of brilliant intensity—that is unlike anything he has ever seen.

"And over there lies the house of my brother Austin." Emily points in the other direction, towards a path that leads off into a small woods.

"He lives next door now?"

"Yes. He has gone East."

Wadsworth pauses a moment, looks at the sun, gazes for a moment at the panoramic view of the Connecticut River valley, glances in the direction she has pointed, and looks back to her, puzzled.

TWELVE

"But I don't understand," he says.

"Understand what?" She is smiling slightly. There is a decided bulge under her lower lip that makes her face plain, but it disappears when she smiles and brings out the beauty of her eyes.

"We are looking south down the river valley, are we not?"

"Yes," she agrees.

"Well, if that is south, then *that*"—and here he points to the right, in the direction of the other house—"must be *west*, not east."

"I am aware of that," she tells him, quite agreeably.

"But you said he went *east*."

"Yes, but I said *East*. With a capital E. Didn't you hear it?"

"Ah. You said it with a capital E."

"Yes, I did."

He regards her in silence for a moment. Then he bursts out laughing. "Miss Dickinson . . ." he says.

"What?" She stops and looks over toward him. Despite her best efforts, the traces of a smile are tugging up the corners of her lips.

"In Amherst, does one use a capital letter to denote opposites?"

"Of course not," she replies. She bends down beside Carlo and scratches him behind his shaggy ears.

Wadsworth stands there, admiring her slim figure, enjoying the slightly old-fashioned cut of her clothes, which makes him feel suddenly, by contrast, rather daring and sophisticated.

"Miss Dickinson," he asks, "does the capital E have a religious significance, perhaps?"

"Of course," she replies. She picks a tick from Carlo's neck and tosses it towards the woods.

"In other words, your brother Austin has found a blissful state."

"Yes."

"He is, in fact, married. He has gone East into paradise."

"Exactly."

"So I have broken your code."

"All communication is a code." She does not look up at him.

He strolls across the side yard and admires the view of the valley.

"Well, shall we walk?" Emily calls to him. "I should be glad to show you my haunts."

"Where you find your trillium and your lady's slipper?"

She comes up beside him. "Yes. Though of course many of the flowers are either past—like the arbutus—or not yet out—like the Cardinal flower."

"It matters not. Lead on, MacDuff."

Side by side, they proceed around to the front of the house, past the oak trees and the evergreen hedge, and cross Main Street to enter the meadow.

"You can see how many other Daisies there are who follow the sun," she comments. The meadow sparkles with hundreds of daisies, shaking their white faces in the summer breeze.

"I know but one," he remarks. "And though she lives in New England—not that far in truth from the sun of Philadelphia—still, sometimes it seems that we are oceans apart."

For several minutes they walk without speaking a word. As Carlo trots along beside them or gallops ahead to check out a rabbit or squirrel (and once, a butterfly), they take their unhurried steps through the tall, waving grass and the billowing sea of daisies. The sky is a dull blue, washed clean by the storms of the previous few days; the grass blows silver and gray in the gusts of wind. They cross the meadow, skirt to the right of the hat factory, and come upon the railroad tracks.

"Here runs our epic," she tells him. He takes her hand and helps her across the tracks; then, by mutual and silent agreement, they let their hands fall apart. Again she feels the memory of his touch, gentle and insistent.

"The swamp lies over here," she says, with a nod of her head. "The yellow violets are still blooming. Do you mind getting your soles damp?"

"A dry soul can offer nothing to God," he replies.

She leads him into the swamp, choosing a path through the higher ground. They do not speak. Frogs chirrup and bark around them; in some of the larger puddles, swarms of little fish stir in sudden ripples over the surface, like quick gusts of wind. They are approaching one of her holy spots. She feels the sun taking her soul and lifting its petals sweetly open. There is no need of words.

The violets are blooming. She stops before the small bank where they grow in a cluster, and nods.

"How beautiful," he says. He crouches down before them. "What lovely, perfect little faces they have. The black markings—so exquisite." Carlo comes up beside him and paws at the mud. He looks up at Wadsworth with a question in his eyes.

She walks on, knowing he will follow.

Entering the woods, they follow the trail past the columbine and adder's tongues, past the hulking white ecstasy of a puffball, towards Rattlesnake Gutter. They move in silence. Shafts of sunlight fall at their feet. Shadows flow across them. Somewhere above them angels surely are flying. The sky through the trees is silver and gold. Heaven is descending on the Earth. All is still around them. Now and then a rock comes free and bounces and tumbles down the hill ahead of them. Carlo has fallen behind somewhere.

She stops at the bottom of the hill and leads him to a narrow gulch. They walk about fifty yards and stop.

"Here," she says.

She gestures towards a colony of small flowers, each with a white stem and a single, nodding flower, bravely lifting their heads towards a distant hope, the sun. In the shadows of the forest, they glow with a spectral shimmer, as if illuminated from within. This light is holy for her. It is the light of dreams, the light of legend, the light of poetry.

"Extraordinary," he exclaims softly. "What are they?"

"They are called Indian pipes."

Now is the time. If she wishes to claim him, now is the time she must step in close to him, turn her petals to the sun, and await his kiss. Then one of three things will happen: either he will awaken from the spell she has cast over him—remembering his wife, his child, his career; or she will awaken from the spell he has cast over her—remembering her obligations to her parents and her desire to be good; or the two of them will proclaim their love and, in that holiest of spots, vanquish the conditions of their earthly and heavenly fire. If that happens, his career as a minister is over, at least in any major city in America, and her life with her family will come to an end. They will be forced to flee to the wilderness, like heroes in a Nathaniel Hawthorne romance, or to one of the territories in the southwest, like common outlaws. Emily Dickinson's great poetry—if she writes great poetry, if she writes poetry at all—will describe alabaster canyons in the desert moonlight, the splendid fat solitude of cactus, the whirring evanescence of a lizard's tongue. She will bear many children and raise them in the untutored west by the light of her New England independence and love of culture. Though she and Charles Wadsworth will remain notorious and disgraced in the East, their grandchildren will remember them as the kindest, most intelligent and altogether most amusing people ever to live on Earth. The small mission church Wadsworth founds will one day be great; the poetry she composes on God and religious doubts will be enshrined as the voice of a true seeker. Their love for each other will remain strong, and they will die happy, unafraid and unrepentant.

But she does not step forward, she does not turn her petals to the sun, she does not claim him. The moment passes.

On the way back he asks, "And as for the assignment you accepted from me?"

She smiles. "I haven't completed it yet, for my flowers don't speak to you."

"The want may be in me, not in you."

"I have something to show you before you leave."

Two faces watch them from the front parlor, then disappear quickly, as Emily and Wadsworth labor up the stairs and continue, slightly winded, onto the front lawn. A bird is hopping about on the walk; it sees them coming, chirps once, and flies off. The rise and fall of its wings are like the fanning oars of a boat in a heavenly sea. "Please come in just for a moment," she says. She pushes open the door and steps inside. "Hello?" she calls.

"Is that you, Emily?" Vinnie asks. She comes sheepishly out of the back hall.

"Of course. You remember Reverend Wadsworth?"

"Good afternoon," he says, lifting his hat.

"This is a pleasant surprise," Vinnie remarks, looking neither pleased nor surprised. She glances from Emily to Wadsworth and back again to Emily. "Well, I'm afraid I must get to my cooking."

"As you wish, Vinnie," Emily says. When Vinnie leaves, she tells Wadsworth, "Wait here for a minute. I'll be right back." She runs up the stairs with her light steps and returns a few minutes later with a small wooden chest.

"Come quickly," she fairly whispers, leading him through the front parlor and into the back parlor. She glances around behind her, with a quick, stealthy motion that makes him smile.

She sits down on a sofa and lifts the top of the chest.

"I haven't told anyone else about these, and I must swear you to secrecy."

"So sworn," he replies.

She pulls out a small, hand-sewn manuscript.

"These are called fascicles. You see, I am collecting my poems. I have already finished two of these little books."

"May I look through them?"

"No—not now, maybe some other time."

"Why have you told no one else?"

"Because, Master, I fear I have not yet fulfilled the assignment."

"You will. You are stronger than you realize, and I have no doubt you can be mighty, if you like."

She accepts his words into her heart.

"I must hide this away before Vinnie sees," she announces breathlessly. She places the little book back in the chest, closes the lid, and runs back upstairs.

"It mustn't be five more years," she tells him as they stand together, unwilling to part, outside the front door. Already they are faces on two decks, on ships bound for separate shores.

"This fall," he says.

"What do you mean?"

"You know that the Colemans have moved to Middletown, Connecticut?"

"Yes."

"I promised to visit Lyman this fall."

"And?"

"And you can visit Eliza."

She looks up into his eyes, searching. His eyes are golden, not brown.

They part without words. They exchange simple silver crucifixes. Her dark eyes glow; his golden brown eyes look saddened. And now, for the first time that day, they shake hands. She will feel his gentle touch for months, for years. The ocean is very wide.

That night Emily sits in her room and looks out over the valley and thinks of her strange, dear Master, her Philadelphia. At her freckled breast, she clutches the crucifix that he has given her. She needs no other sign.

Margaret talks, of course. Vinnie wants to keep silent on the subject, but eventually she is forced to tell her parents before they hear it from others. They are horrified to learn of the unauthorized visit and the unescorted walk outside. (Carlo does not count as an escort.) Emily doesn't care. She has touched his hand lightly, three times. That is all. That is her taste of heaven.

THIRTEEN

Autumn, 1860

In August of 1860, waiting for the trip to Connecticut to materialize—and still hardly daring to hope that she will see Wadsworth there—Emily writes a sweet poem about misery and love.

> *If you were coming in the Fall,*
> *I'd brush the Summer by*
> *With half a smile, and half a spurn,*
> *As Housewives do, a Fly.*
>
> *If I could see you in a year,*
> *I'd wind the months in balls –*
> *And put them each in separate Drawers,*
> *For fear the numbers fuse –*

During the carriage ride down the Connecticut River valley from Amherst to Middletown—a distance of about fifty miles—Emily is between laughter and tears.

"Emily, what in the world is wrong with you?" Vinnie asks.

"With me?"

"Yes, with you."

"Nothing. There's nothing wrong with me." Emily turns her head to watch the trees streaming by.

"Nothing that you wish to share, anyway."

Emily doesn't reply.

Vinnie has her suspicions. Though she hasn't read them and Emily won't discuss them, she knows about the letters. She saw Wadsworth that day. She is well aware of the whispering in the village after not just one, but several people, saw Emily walk off into the swamp with a handsome and distinguished-looking stranger. She has had to reassure Mother and Father that Emily is not about to run off with a married man. They have encouraged this visit to the Colemans partly as a way of getting their intense older daughter out of the house. Everyone in the family thinks it will do Emily good; it will stabilize her emotions and perhaps restore her reason if she pays a visit to her sensible friend Eliza.

Emily is excited and afraid. From the letters they have been exchanging, she knows what none of her family does, that Charles Wadsworth will be there. She also senses—just why, she can't say—that he is coming to say good-bye.

"Oh, my darling, don't you look wonderful!" Eliza Coleman exclaims to Emily after welcoming her relative Eudocia Flynt. "And Vinnie, aren't you the beauty!" Eliza herself is flushed with youthful beauty and happiness—her cheeks are full of color, her blue eyes sparkle, and her blond hair is pulled prettily back in a way that gives her just a hint of the matronly.

"If I have any beauty remaining, you're the only one who has noticed," Vinnie replies. In her late twenties, Vinnie has begun to take on the bitterness and cynicism that will accent her later years.

"I was shocked to hear of Joseph's marriage to Laura Baker," Eliza sympathizes. "I thought you two were perfect for one another."

"Let's not talk of it," Vinnie replies. "I understand you have happier news."

"Yes—John and I have chosen a date—June sixth, in Monson."

"What a lovely time of year," Emily comments. "The bees will be out, and the daisies will be dancing, and cardinals will sing their sweet vespers for you."

"You're among friends," Vinnie reminds her. "You don't need to try to impress anyone with your poetic verses."

"I know I can't impress you no matter what I do."

"Then don't try."

"My, it must have been a pleasant ride in the carriage," Eliza comments.

"Juliet here is laughing one minute and crying the next and won't talk about it with me. Maybe you'll do better with her," Vinnie replies.

"Well, why don't you two go freshen up," Eliza suggests.

Emily doesn't even have to ask: Charles Wadsworth is not there yet.

FOURTEEN

As they gather for dinner that night, a storm rolls in; lightning flashes, thunder mutters and growls, and a sudden deafening downpour almost drowns out their conversation. "Not a very nice night for traveling," Lyman Coleman observes. "Ladies, I don't know if you know him, but we were expecting a friend of ours tonight. Charles Wadsworth. Oh, yes, you do know Reverend Wadsworth—he preached that Sunday in March four or five years ago when you visited us, if you remember."

"I think we remember him," Vinnie says.

Emily can feel Eliza watching her carefully, and she tries to show no reaction to the terrible words, *"were* expecting."

"Is he not coming then, Father?" Eliza asks. Emily knows Eliza is asking the question for her benefit, and she watches silently.

"Well, I'm not sure. He's been promising me that he

will come tonight—we've had it planned for weeks—
but of course if the roads are too wet he may have to
stop in Old Lyme. This roast beef is delicious. I always
said, the longer aged, the sweeter on the tongue."

"I am told that men think the same of women,"
Vinnie comments.

"Oh, really?" Lyman replies politely.

"Yes," Vinnie says. "But of course, the truth is, the
longer in the tooth, the harsher the bite."

"Oh, hush," Eliza tells her.

The evening passes drearily for Emily. She is too
agitated to sit and knit, as Eliza is doing, and she has
not the heart for the wry witticisms that Vinnie is fling-
ing in the direction of anyone willing to listen. She gets
out of her seat often and stands by the window, waiting
for the face of heaven to distill itself from the empty
black night. By nine o'clock there is still no sign of him.

She feels almost relieved in a way that he has not
come. It strains her nerves so much merely to think of
him, she is not sure she has the strength to see him in
person.

Mr. and Mrs. Coleman have already gone upstairs
for the night, Emily and Eliza are finishing their last
cup of tea, and Vinnie is snoring loudly in one of the
downstairs bedrooms, when there is a commotion

outside and a brisk knock at the door. Eliza runs to the door, followed at a few yards' distance by Emily, and pulls the door open.

"Why, come in this instant!" she calls. "My poor Reverend Wadsworth, you are drenched!"

"Thank you," he manages to say.

"You have lost your voice too."

"It is nothing." He takes off his hat and pulls off his traveler's cloak. "I must apologize for being so late," he rasps.

"Don't apologize. You have caught a cold."

"No, my voice does this sometimes." He is fairly whispering now.

"Is your horse being attended to?"

"Yes, your man already has him well in hand." He glances about the room. "Ah," he says, seeing Emily, who has withdrawn to the far side of the room like a timid bird. "And your parents?" he asks Eliza.

"I am afraid they have already retired for the night. They don't stay awake beyond nine o'clock anymore."

"I'm dreadfully sorry to be so late. It was the weather. Perhaps I may see them at breakfast?"

"It hurts me to hear your voice. Could I offer you something—perhaps some tea?"

"Tea would be very nice," he whispers.

Eliza takes him by the hand and walks him into the room. He stops and looks toward Emily, who stands silently against the opposite wall, staring at him with eyes darker than sherry. His face is pale, and a muscle in his right cheek is quivering slightly. He looks towards her without speaking, and she knows. Immediately she knows. His recent letters have forecast the finest point on this moment.

"Would you like tea also, Emily?"

"No, thank you, Eliza."

Eliza leaves the room with a promise to return shortly.

"Good evening," Emily says to him.

"Good evening. If such an evening can be called good."

"Any evening that holds your face is a blessed evening." Already she is fighting off the tears. She turns her head. "Why?" she asks.

"Why what?" he queries, puzzled.

"I can't tell you."

"Yes you can. Tell me of the want. And I will do what I can." He walks up to her and stands in front of her.

Emily glances up at him. "Why do you look at me this way, and why have I known all day in my heart what is coming?"

He looks at her in silence for a while, and then says, "Emily, we have much to discuss."

She collapses into a chair. "I can't bear to hear what you are about to say to me." She starts to sob. Large perfectly formed tears roll down her face, the shape of tiny petals. She does nothing to conceal them from him. It is the second time in a week that a woman he loves has cried openly before him.

Eliza Coleman walks smiling into the room, carrying a silver tray on which are arranged tea, cups, sugar, cream, and little silver spoons. She takes in the scene, sets down the tray, and leaves immediately. Her soft footsteps climb the back stairs.

Charles Wadsworth pulls a chair up beside Emily Dickinson.

"I didn't know—for a long time—what your feelings were for me; and more inexcusably, I didn't know—for an even longer time—what my feelings were for you. I read your poetry, of course . . . but . . . well, perhaps I've always been slow to understand matters of the heart."

Emily listens in silence. The tears are still rolling down her cheeks, each one a mere drop in a vast ocean.

"Why didn't you come to me In White earlier?" he asks.

"What do you mean?" Her voice is small and distant. For now, her tears have slowed.

"Why didn't you tell me all—confess to me your feelings of love before God, so that I could know?"

"I did confess. I sent you my flowers."

He moves a bit closer and tries to console her with a term of endearment that he has used, up till now, only in their letters. "Daisy, your poetry is unique. It's remarkable. But it is brilliant and complex and full of shadowy depths, and I would hardly call it a confession of love."

She turns toward him. Her eyes glow with an intense light that he finds disquieting. "Has anyone ever loved someone more or been more true to them than I have been to you for five long years?" She is crying harder again.

"I thought for a long time that it was the love a pupil feels for her Master."

"You knew it was more than that."

"Perhaps." He takes a breath and lets it out. "Perhaps I knew. Perhaps, in my weakness, I was too flattered by your expressions of affection to ask you to stop."

Emily stands up, takes a napkin from the serving tray, and wipes her face dry. "My love for you grew quickly, more quickly than you knew," she admits. "But over time, you had to know that you had become dearer and dearer to me. That you had become my heavenly Master." She looks at him. Her eyes are so childlike and direct, he feels a shiver in his soul. "Everything I did was with you in mind."

He recoils slightly, dismayed by the anguish in her voice. "What did you wish from me?" he asks.

"I don't know. Redemption, I suppose."

He leans forward again. "Redemption? For someone who is not a true believer? For someone who has held back from giving herself completely to Christ? What kind of redemption could I give you?"

She meets his gaze. "Redemption from myself."

"Redemption from yourself? How can that be?"

"I can't explain it. But I know it can be." She shakes her head and gazes off into some impenetrable depths of darkness.

"I am wounded," she says after a minute.

"Wounded? How?"

"Because of what I felt . . . and what you didn't."

"What do you mean?"

"I felt the oceans in me move at your command, I felt our connection across all the time and space that stood between us, while you . . . you felt none of that?"

He looks at her in silence. She returns his gaze for a minute, then lowers her eyes.

"You would rather not speak the truth," she murmurs.

"I don't know how to begin."

"You might begin with this: What were your feelings for me?" she asks drily.

It is a few moments before he replies. He speaks slowly, at first in a whisper, but his voice seems to gain power as he goes on. "I didn't realize for the longest time that I had fallen in love with you. If I had realized, I would have stopped writing to you, I would have called it all off."

"And why didn't you realize?"

"I was entranced, I suppose. The power of your mind is remarkable and quite beautiful to me. I allowed myself to go farther along than I ever should have."

"Then you were wounded, too, perhaps?"

"No, it was more . . . I was obsessed. I allowed myself to think of you at each moment of the day, and refer my earthly happiness to the thought of you. I became filled with the image of you. You changed the world somehow for me. And all this was wrong, because I had already given my life to someone else."

"I knew that."

"Then why did you continue to write me as you did?" he asks.

"I didn't think of her often, but when I did, I suppose I hoped she would go away," Emily answers, with a fleeting smile.

"But she hasn't gone away. And two very bad things have happened."

"What?" Her voice is tiny again.

"The first involved an anonymous letter. From someone who signed herself 'AS.' Do you know such a person?"

"I expect it was our darling neighbor Abby Sweetser."

"Several weeks ago she wrote a letter to my wife introducing herself as an upstanding member of the Amherst community, and she rather gleefully described our walk through the swamp. She made it sound much more salacious than it was, but she included enough detail to make it convincing. This raised my wife's suspicions, but she said nothing to me. Then the second thing happened. Jane intercepted some mail for me from Mrs. Holland."

"Oh no."

"And she read your poem about the Daisy. *'The Daisy follows soft the Sun – And when his golden walk is done – Sits Shily at his feet – He – waking – finds the flower there – Wherefore – Marauder – art thou here? Because, Sir, love is sweet!'* My wife is a very astute reader. She knew exactly what it meant."

"And she confronted you?"

"Not for a few days. We have a new baby in the family—our darling little Charles—and she has been quite busy between Edith and Charles. Then finally one night she did confront me."

"And?"

"And I told her I would call off our friendship."

"Is that all?"

"No. She said we must move. She, I, and our children must move."

"Where?"

"Far away."

"How far?"

He looks at her gently. "I have friends in San Francisco who have been trying for years to call me to their church—their minister is too controversial. They will need someone in about a year."

"No!"

"The Calvary church. It may not come to pass. But if they call me, I will go."

She turns away and starts to sob again. Now her whole body convulses with her desolation. "Oh, it is too cruel!" she cries. "It is too heartless. I would never see you again!"

"I am sorry. But it would be best for both of us. Not to mention my family."

"I will still write you," she says fiercely. "I will write you through Eliza so your wife doesn't suspect. I don't care if you never read my letters. I must write to you still!"

She turns to him and throws herself upon him. She snuggles her head against his shoulder and pulls herself violently to him. He feels that an ocean has swept over him. He has never felt the force of a fury so strong. She is hugging him so tightly he wonders if she will pass through his skin and take residence in his body.

Gradually, her sobs subside. She grows still. The stillness seems to last for a long time. Then, somehow, she is sitting on his knee and looking into his eyes. It is almost as if they are drifting in and out of sleep, but they are together, and awake.

Slowly—neither of them knows how it begins or whose fatal idea it is—they turn their heads and kiss—just once, lightly. And then again. Softly, sweetly, she kisses him again and again in a way he has never felt before, and a wild ecstasy pulses into him. The night seems to exist outside time and space, on some strange shore. She takes his hand and leads him into the spare bedroom where he will be staying.

"What are we doing?" he asks.

"If I am never to see you again, Master, I must have this. Here, Master, is the way to heal the wound." She kisses his face, his eyes, she brings her tongue back to his lips and opens his shirt and touches the hair on his chest.

"Does this shaggier vest feel anything so great as the love in my breast?" she asks.

"It does," he admits.

"Then show me."

FIFTEEN

1860 – 1861

In their first meeting, Wadsworth had confided to Emily that his life was full of "dark secrets."

The darkest of these secrets was that in his youth, like thousands of his fellow countrymen in the mid-1800's, he contracted the great plague of the time—from a prostitute while he was in college. He later transferred this plague to his unknowing wife Jane, who suffered multiple stillbirths until the disease finally entered the "latent" stage, allowing her to return to full health and finally produce healthy offspring twelve years into the marriage.

We know this plague by the name syphilis. Until the discovery of penicillin, it was incurable.

In Wadsworth, the plague had left permanent scars on his face and would eventually weaken irreparably his heart and respiratory system. But for now, with him, as with Jane, it was in its latent stage.

Once syphilis has entered the "latent" stage, it is not contagious unless the carrier of the disease bears an open sore that allows blood-to-blood contact.

Normally, Wadsworth would not carry such a sore, and the plague could not be transferred to a sexual partner.

But after the terrible last few weeks with his wife— her recriminations, her bitter tears, his apology and promise to call off the relationship with Emily—they realized the night before he was to leave on his trip to Connecticut that they'd had no intimate contact for almost a month.

Jane had been having "feminine troubles" for more than a week, and she wished to be accommodating to her husband (and take the edge off any possible lust) before he left. Victorian wives were not prudes: they dealt (albeit as secretly as possible) with the diseases which their husbands transmitted to them as a result of alliances with infected prostitutes; they put up with stillbirths and miscarriages; they were willing and passionate partners in connubial bliss and were, if anything, less squeamish about the physical side of life than most Americans today.

So it happened, on the night of October seventeenth, that Jane Wadsworth took the minister's pleasure in her hands and caressed and stroked him towards release. Her hands were rough from washing, from changing children's underclothes, from baking and scrubbing and sweeping. Maybe, in the lingering anger she felt toward her husband, she stroked him harder and with more haste than usual as she led him towards climax and herself towards sleep. She certainly was unaware, and he was in too much pleasure to protest the slight sting of pain, as her thumb rubbed a tiny raw spot, just below the head. Neither of them had any idea what this would mean. As his hand sought the warmth and softness of her maternal breast, he spurted out his manly gratitude and confessed that he loved her.

The next morning, Jane helped him pack his things. She was cheerful again and affectionate. She was pretty and resourceful. Once she pressed her hand to his forehead and asked if he was feeling all right. He thought so. It was as though he were sleepwalking. He could barely feel the sore; it only bothered him when he turned quickly and his clothing chafed his skin. It would be red and a little oozy that night.

❧

Two nights later, Emily would fall back on the bed and pull him onto her and whisper into his ear, "Yes. Yes. Yes, my Love. Now, my Philadelphia."

❧

On the morning of October twentieth, Wadsworth breakfasts with Mr. and Mrs. Coleman and prepares to ride to New Haven for a meeting on church finances.

He holds court on the front threshold, giving his farewells. He says good-bye to the Colemans, who then wander off around the carriage, looking at the horse and the way his bags are tied on and commenting on this and that.

Emily is standing in the hallway. She looks calm and still—a forced tranquility. Her eyes glow towards him with an unwavering orange flame.

He takes a step back inside. "God be with you," he says.

"And with you," she replies.

He takes two more steps, three more, and he is beside her. He takes her hand. "I will never forget."

She drinks deeply of his eyes, but she says nothing. Her hand presses his. She gives no other sign.

"I must go," he tells her. He lets go of her hand, turns, and walks away. This time, he too will remember her touch, though twenty long years apart will be wound in balls, and put each in separate drawers, before they meet again.

Despair has not yet settled over her. Almost every other emotion is warring inside her; none can win. She goes through her daily routine and thinks of everything and nothing at once. The despair will come.

About a week later, early one morning while squatting over the chamber pot, she discovers the small, painless sore. Over the next week the chancre grows a bit in size, blooms to a redder hue, fades like a dying coal, and disappears.

It is nothing.

Three weeks later, she comes down with a fever and develops a pale rose-colored rash on her feet and hands. She takes to her bed and remains there for several weeks that winter. Vinnie attends to Emily, notices the rash, checks the fever, and draws her conclusions. For the time being she says nothing. For as long as possible, she will protect her sister from the truth.

In January of 1861, just emerging from her fever and still unaware that she has the pox, Emily writes the second Master letter.

Master

If you saw a bullet hit a Bird – and he told you he was'nt shot – you might weep at his courtesy, but you would certainly doubt his word.

One drop more from the gash that stains your Daisy's bosom – then would you believe? Thomas' faith in Anatomy, was stronger than his faith in faith. God made me – Master – I did'nt be – myself. I don't know how it was done. He built the heart in me – Bye and bye it outgrew me – and like the little mother – with the big child – I got tired holding him. I heard of a thing called "Redemption" – which rested men and women. You remember I asked you for it – you gave me

*something else. I forgot the Redemption – I did'nt tell you for
a long time, but I knew you had altered me – and was tired
no more –*

> *No Rose, yet felt myself a'bloom,*
> *No Bird – yet rode in Ether.*

*I am older – tonight, Master – but the love is the same
– so are the moon and the crescent. If it had been God's will
that I might breathe where you breathed – and find the place
– myself – at night – if I never forget that I am not with you
– and that sorrow and frost are nearer than I – if I wish with
a might I cannot repress – that mine were the Queen's place
– the love of the Plantagenet is my only apology – To come
nearer than presbyteries – and nearer than the new Coat –
that the Tailor made – the prank of the Heart at play on the
Heart – in holy Holiday – is forbidden me – You make me say
it over – I fear you laugh – when I do not see – "Chillon" is
not funny. Have you the Heart in your breast – Sir – is it set
like mine – a little to the left – has it the misgiving – if it wake
in the night – perchance – itself to it – a timbrel is it – itself
to it a tune?*

*These things are holy, Sir, I touch them hallowed, but
persons who pray – dare remark "Father"! You say I do not
tell you all – Daisy confessed – and denied not.*

*Vesuvius don't talk – Etna – don't – one of them – said
a syllable – a thousand years ago, and Pompeii heard it, and
hid forever – She could'nt look the world in the face, after-
ward – I suppose – Bashful Pompeii! "Tell you of the want"
– you know what a leech is, don't you – and Daisy's arm is*

small – and you have felt the horizon hav'nt you – and did the sea – never come so close as to make you dance?

I don't know what you can do for it – thank you – Master – but if I had the Beard on my cheek – like you – and you – had Daisy's petals – and you cared so for me – what would become of you? Could you forget me in fight, or flight – or the foreign land? Could'nt Carlo, and you and I walk in the meadows an hour – and nobody care but the Bobolink – and his – a silver scruple? I used to think when I died – I could see you – so I died as fast as I could – but the "Corporation" are going too so Heaven won't be sequestered – now – Say I may wait for you – say I need go with no stranger to the to me – untried fold – I waited a long time – Master – but I can wait more – wait till my hazel hair is dappled – and you carry the cane – then I can look at my watch and if the Day is too far declined – we can take the chances for heaven – What would you do with me if I came "in white?" Have you the little chest to put the Alive – in?

I want to see you more – Sir – than all I wish for in this world – and the wish – altered a little – will be my only one – for the skies.

Could you come to New England – this summer – would you come to Amherst – Would you like to come – Master?

Would Daisy disappoint you – no – she would'nt – Sir – it were comfort forever – just to look in your face, while you looked in mine – then I could play in the woods till Dark – till you take me where Sundown cannot find us – and the true keep coming – till the town is full.

I did'nt think to tell you, you did'nt come to me "in white," nor ever told me why.

Meanwhile, Wadsworth is actively negotiating with the Calvary Presbyterian Society in San Francisco, expecting to leave for the west coast with his family in September of that year.

☙

In the spring of 1861, Emily recovers her health. She starts to drive herself too hard, too soon. She begins to write poetry again, keeping herself up late at night. She is punishing herself, trying to will herself to be healthier than she really is. She can only view herself in the shattered mirror of her relationship with Wadsworth.

Title divine, is mine.
The Wife without the Sign –
Acute Degree conferred on me –
Empress of Calvary –
Royal, all but the Crown –
Betrothed, without the Swoon
God gives us Women –
When You hold Garnet to Garnet –
Gold – to Gold –
Born – Bridalled – Shrouded –
In a Day –
Tri Victory –
"My Husband" – Women say

Stroking the Melody –
Is this the way –

Vinnie doesn't know what her secretive sister is doing in her room at midnight. But she sees that she is wearing herself out.

Finally, one morning, Vinnie decides that it is time.

By now Emily is well enough to resume her morning chores. She has finished making the bread and is seated in the kitchen, looking through some stray recipe cards. Margaret has not yet arrived for the day.

Vinnie sits opposite her. Emily is pale, and her eyes look larger and rounder than the famous picture of her. She has developed some new mannerisms. She stops sometimes in the middle of a sentence and seems to listen to something, as if to news from the heavens.

"I want to talk to you about your health." Vinnie looks at Emily very directly. Her black hair is pulled back in a bun, and her face looks all business.

"It was silly to be so sick, wasn't it? But thank God it's all over. I suppose it was the shock of this fall. It was my nerves, I think, being strained beyond the breaking point." Emily's eyes flit around the room.

"It was more than nerves," Vinnie tells her.

"What do you mean?"

"Emily, I want you to remember back very carefully to the time before you came down with the illness. Did you happen to notice a patch of raw skin, like a sore, possibly painless—some time before the fever came on?"

For a minute Emily doesn't answer. She has thought of this, of course, from time to time, though she hasn't let herself dwell on it. "Yes, I did," she finally admits.

"In a very sensitive spot?"

"Yes." Emily brings her hand to her cheek.

"And then it cleared up?"

"Entirely. I thought it was nothing."

"And then the fever and the rash."

"Yes."

Vinnie reaches forward and takes her sister's hand. "Do you know what this means?"

She hasn't told the truth to herself, she hasn't wanted to, but somewhere inside she has known.

"I do." Emily looks forward into time and sees illness, life without her Master . . . a bleak landscape, herself and silence wrecked solitary on a distant shore.

"Should I say the word aloud?"

"Please don't. I never want to hear some words—I fear their power."

"With some people, you know, nothing else ever happens."

"So I have heard."

"You may be one of the lucky ones."

"One can only hope."

"But you must moderate your work so as not to exhaust yourself."

Emily slumps forward and puts her head in her arms. Vinnie comes up beside her and puts her arms around her.

"You know I will never leave you alone," Vinnie tells her.

"And Mother and Father?" Emily asks without looking up.

"They suspect nothing. They have no way of knowing. Unless you start to show some other signs."

"They haven't guessed?"

"No." She bends down beside her sister and kisses her tenderly on the cheek.

Emily will keep driving herself, keep writing her poems, no matter what the cost to her health.

A few months later, finally, she forces herself to write one last letter to Wadsworth, hinting delicately at what has happened to her, and he writes back immediately, even more secretly and delicately, on a small piece of notepaper that bears his initials. Trying to shield their intimacy, he deliberately misspells her name.

My Dear Miss Dickenson,

I am distressed beyond measure at your note received this moment, —I can only imagine the affliction which has befallen, or is now befalling you . . . .

I am very, very anxious to learn more definitely of your trial—and though I have no right to intrude upon your sorrows yet I beg you to write me, though it be but a word.

In great haste

Sincerely and most affectionately Yours—

She does not reply right away. He needs no reply. He knows.

Part III

Big my Secret but it's bandaged –

SIXTEEN

1861 – 1864

From 1861 to 1863, Emily Dickinson writes an astonishing amount of poetry, most of it highly accomplished,
much of it new and great: eighty-eight poems in 1861,
two hundred and twenty-seven in 1862, two hundred
and ninety-five in 1863. She creates some of the most
agonized love poems known to the English language,
some of most vigorous and evocative images, and some
of the most cryptic and complex lines of argument. As
she reels from the shock of having and losing Wadsworth, she will simultaneously die and heal herself,
lose her voice and rediscover it in pain, and rise finally
to the glory of survival.

Though a number of her poems mention secrets
and a secret love, one in particular, written in 1862 —
seven years after her first meeting with Wadsworth —

describes the burden, both emotional and physical, that she is carrying.

Rearrange a "Wife's" Affection!
When they dislocate my Brain!
Amputate my freckled Bosom!
Make me bearded like a man!

Blush, my spirit, in thy Fastness –
Blush, my unacknowledged clay –
Seven years of troth have taught thee
More than Wifehood ever may!

Love that never leaped it's socket –
Trust intrenched in narrow pain –
Constancy thro' fire – awarded –
Anguish – bare of anodyne!

Burden – borne so far triumphant –
None suspect me of the crown,
For I wear the "Thorns" till Sunset –
Then – my Diadem put on.

Big my Secret but it's bandaged –
It will never get away
Till the Day it's Weary Keeper
Leads it through the Grave to thee.

The bandaged secret she will lead back to Wadsworth after death is not only the love, but the illness that they share.

As the date for Wadsworth's journey to San Francisco approaches, she drafts the third of her Master letters, an expression of her terrible pain and need.

Oh, did I offend it – Did'nt it want me to tell it the truth – Daisy – offend it – who bends her smaller life to his meeker every day – who only asks – a task – something to do for love of it – some little way she cannot guess to make that master glad –

A love so big it scares her, rushing among her small heart – pushing aside the blood and leaving her faint and white in the gust's arm –

Daisy – who never flinched thro' that awful parting, but held her life so tight he should not see the wound – who would have sheltered him in her childish bosom – only it was'nt big eno' for a Guest so large – this Daisy – grieve her Lord – and yet it often blundered – Perhaps she grieved his taste – perhaps her odd-Backwoodsman ways teased his finer nature. Daisy knows all that – but must she go unpardoned – teach her, preceptor grace – teach her majesty – Slow at patrician things – Even the wren upon her nest learns more than Daisy dares –

Low at the knee that bore her once unto wordless rest Daisy kneels a culprit – tell her her fault – Master – if it is small eno' to cancel with her life, she is satisfied – but punish don't banish her – shut her in prison, Sir – only pledge that you will forgive – sometime – before the grave, and Daisy will not mind – She will awake in your likeness.

Wonder stings me more than the Bee – who did never sting me – but made gay music with his might wherever I did go – Wonder wastes my pound, you said I had no size to spare –

You send the water over the Dam in my brown eyes –

I've got a cough as big as a thimble – but I don't care for that – I've got a Tomahawk in my side but that don't hurt me much. Her master stabs her more –

Wont he come to her – or will he let her seek him, never minding so long wandering if to him at last.

Oh how the sailor strains, when his boat is filling – Oh how the dying tug, till the angel comes, Master – open your life wide, and take me in forever, I will never be tired – I will never be noisy when you want to be still. I will be your best little girl – nobody else will see me, but you – but that is enough – I shall not want any more – and all that Heaven only will disappoint me – will be because it's not so dear

For days she wrestles with herself. Should she send this abject letter, with its offer to give up her very selfhood? Or should she not send it and thereby condemn herself to silence? Her soul is suspended between two impossible poles. Finally she folds the letter perfectly in thirds and puts it forever away.

SEVENTEEN

Near the end of 1862, Emily first notices that bright light sears her eyes. The day of the first snowfall, after going outside in the dazzling sunlight, she stumbles back into the front hall, crying out in pain.

"It's my eyes," she gasps to Vinnie, who comes running.

Vinnie leads her into the front parlor. Through the window, Vinnie catches a glimpse of the unblemished face of newly fallen snow, while Emily, her eyes clenched shut, is surrounded by the nightmarish features of swirling darkness.

"Sit down."

Emily obeys her sister and takes a seat on the divan.

"What's happening to you?" Vinnie asks.

"I don't know. I was out in the snow and something happened."

"What happened?"

"The darkness came."

Vinnie gazes into her sister's face. "You'll be all right. You just need to sit awhile." She glances out the window again at the crisp, flawless sheet of snow. She pats her sister's hand.

"It's nothing," Emily murmurs.

Vinnie narrows her eyes. "This isn't the first time, is it?"

"No," Emily admits.

"How long has this been happening?"

"For a few weeks. Here and there. But never like this." Emily has opened one eye. Her sister's face bobs before her, ridiculously close and far away at the same time, and grossly misshapen, like something seen through a slab of ice. Then the light floods over her again, and the world swirls in darkness, vast and molten.

Over the next weeks her despair grows more intense. She writes a poem about the coming of this second night—both the night of pain and rejection by a lover, and the night of growing darkness.

The first Day's Night had come –
And grateful that a thing
So terrible – had been endured –
I told my Soul to sing –

She said her strings were snapt –
Her bow – to atoms blown –

And so to mend her – gave me work
Until another Morn –

And then – a Day as huge
As Yesterdays in pairs,
Unrolled it's horror in my face –
Until it blocked my eyes . . .

Early in 1863, the pain intensifies. For longer and longer periods of time, Emily needs to retire to a darkened room.

"Vinnie, what is happening with your sister?" Father asks one afternoon. He has just returned from his day at Amherst College, where he is Treasurer of the institution.

"She has decided to repair to her room and read for the rest of the day," Vinnie answers carefully.

"Her bookish ways will be the end of her." Edward stands there, as still and hard as uncut diamond. Mother has taken her place silently beside him, and now she speaks in her soft alto voice.

"She didn't have a book with her."

Vinnie throws up a hand. "Oh, Emily has books everywhere." She turns and walks away. "I will check on her."

Early the next morning Mother, with uncharacteristic forthrightness, confronts Vinnie outside the back door.

"Something is wrong with Emily," she murmurs.

Vinnie looks at her. "Yes, Mother."

"Her eyes?"

"Yes," Vinnie admits.

Mother tightens her lips. "I will tell your father."

Unseen by either of them, Emily is within earshot. She still gets up at dawn each day and starts the bread, and then she comes out to work in the garden while the dough is rising. She has only an hour or so each morning before the light grows too bright for her eyes to bear.

Crouching behind a rose bush, she hears her mother's words. She deadheads one flower, and then another, and slumps forward. Two miseries flow over her, the misery of her affliction and the misery of its being discovered.

Late that summer a doctor from Boston, a renowned eye specialist, pays a house call. He strolls up the front steps with a refined swagger, sweating not a bit despite the closeness and heat of the day. He comes inside, unpacks his instruments, struts about, and asks to see the patient.

A few minutes later there is a soft footfall on the stairs, and Emily traipses into the front parlor, her head down, with the air of a prisoner being led to the gallows. She looks at the doctor once, gives a brief replica of a smile, and seats herself. He regards her from his imperial male heights.

He begins to examine her, and his manner changes, becomes simpler and more confiding somehow, while still remaining businesslike. He shines a light in her eyes—making a reassuring, sympathetic sound at her whimpers of pain—and peers through a silver instrument into her eyes, first the left, then the right. He asks her to look up, then down, then to the left and to the right. He introduces a drop of liquid into each eye, tells her to sit quietly for fifteen minutes, then examines her eyes again.

She is heartened by the gentle force of the examination; she glances over at him and is disarmed by the peaceful, intelligent glimmer in his gray-green eyes. He is kind and graceful and has an elegant but masculine manner that quickens something inside her. She knows he can make her better. She raises her head, looks at him again, and taking her cue from him, she stands up and glides silently away.

The doctor and Edward go for a walk in the meadow. Emily watches breathless through the window as they stroll about and converse. Edward is gesticulating wildly—apparently arguing with the doctor. The doctor, hands clasped behind his back, walks calmly on. Eventually they stop at the far side of the meadow and stand talking. They turn and retrace their steps to the Homestead.

Emily excuses herself from taking dinner.

That night after dinner Edward remains alone in

the front parlor. He is not reading over his legal briefs or looking through a magazine or book. He is not looking out the window. He is just sitting, and he stays there until quite late. Finally, he trudges up the stairs to join his wife in bed. As he makes the turn to the second floor, Emily stumbles out of Vinnie's room, eyes red and swollen, her hair long and uncombed. He stops and bows his head slightly. All the color is gone from his face. He has been stunned too deeply for words. He seems unable to move.

Trembling, Emily kneels before him. Gently, he touches her hair with his right hand, feeling the silky flow of her tresses on his fingers as if for the first time in his life. She seizes his left hand, twisted and gnarled now like the root of an old tree, and brings it to her face. For a moment she rests her cheek against the rough back of his hand. Then she turns and runs into her room and closes the door.

He will say nothing to her of her affliction, not for all the years that remain.

❧

The darkness overtaking her has the paradoxical effect of focusing her thoughts to the sharpness and brilliance of diamonds. The heat and pressure of loving and losing Wadsworth has morphed the coal of her being into the hardest, most dense gem imaginable. The blindness that Wadsworth has inadvertently given her has flooded her inner vision with light and suffused her soul with a terrible greatness.

> *There is a pain – so utter –*
> *It swallows substance up –*
> *Then covers the Abyss with Trance –*
> *So Memory can step*
> *Around – across – opon it –*
> *As One within a Swoon –*
> *Goes safely – where an open eye –*
> *Would drop Him – Bone by Bone –*

EIGHTEEN

For seven months in 1864 and six months in 1865, Emily lived in Cambridge with her cousins, Louisa and Frances Norcross, and received treatment for her eyes from the eminent eye doctor who had visited her at the Homestead, Henry Willard Williams. No details are known about the medications that he used. The first course of treatment had little effect, but by the end of the second year her vision had improved dramatically. Bright light no longer hurt her eyes, and she was able to work as long as she liked on her poetry without any physical pain.

There were no other symptoms of the disease that had entered her body almost five years earlier except some shortness of breath.

By late 1865 she was able to resume her chores at home. The timing was fortunate, since Margaret had gotten married in October, 1865 and had quit her job with the Dickinsons. Emily and Vinnie had to do the bulk of the household cleaning and cooking. Along with her bread-making abilities, Emily developed skill in making desserts. She earned a reputation for her gingerbread cookies and her puddings.

❧

"What do you think is ailing Carlo?" Emily asks Vinnie one day that November. They are standing in the side yard. Ranks of leaves fall trembling from the sky. Through the thinning trees they have a clear view of the stone-colored siding and green shutters of the Evergreens. The house looks solitary and gloomy at this time of year; lacking the brilliant setting of summer, it seems oddly out of place.

The wind is cold and out of the Northeast. Indian summer has already gone; winter is coming.

"The same thing that's ailing all of us. He's growing older."

"True." Emily has to admit, at age thirty-four she does feel older. Faint lines have begun to etch themselves about her eyes; she has put on a pound or two. She has begun her long, slow descent to Earth. "But he seems sad, almost full of despair."

"He's just a dog, Emily. He doesn't know what despair is."

"Every creature knows despair. Look at him lying on the porch, like a sack of coals."

"He's always looked like a sack of coals lying down."

"What was he like when I was in Cambridge?" Emily asks.

"Very much like this."

"Did you ever walk with him?"

"Emily, he won't walk with anyone but you."

"Carlo!" Emily calls. "Come here, boy! Come here!" She taps her hands on her thighs. "Come on!" Carlo lifts his head in her direction. His tail thumps, once, twice. He places his head back on his paws and stares off into space, hoping he won't be noticed.

"I don't believe he can see me," Emily says. She approaches the dog. "Carlo, where am I?"

The tail thumps again on the wooden floor of the porch. He doesn't lift his head. His big, dimpled black nose wriggles slightly.

She brings her hand in front of his face. He doesn't respond. She jerks her hand toward his nose; he doesn't flinch.

"Oh Carlo!" she says. "You poor, wounded baby! You're living in darkness!" She begins to cry. Kneeling, she places her arms around his big head and hugs him. "Oh, to be plunged into darkness and to have no one even know!"

The sack of coals sniffs at Emily's hair and patiently licks her face.

Carlo's health rapidly grows worse. By December

he has stopped eating on his own. Emily brings him inside, and Father doesn't protest. The huge old dog lies at the back of the kitchen, on a bed she fashions out of old flour sacks and pillows. He smells like a blanket that once soaked, never dried properly.

She sits beside him, knitting or sometimes writing a verse. From time to time she heats milk and spoons it into his mouth. As the weeks advance she has to hold his mouth open to make him swallow. His large red tongue is sleepy and unwilling to work. But his tail still thumps when she calls his name.

"How is he?" Father asks one night in January as she tends to the dog.

"Not well."

Father stands there, erect and spare, his wreath of thinning grey hair catching the light of the oil lamps.

"I don't suppose a doctor could help."

"Thank you, Father. I don't think a doctor could help now."

"He's been a real friend, hasn't he?"

"For fifteen years."

Father turns, as if to go. "Well, it's all a part of life. Even with people."

"It's not a part of life that I can bear."

"You seem to enjoy tending to him."

"The tending I don't mind. It's the prospect of parting."

Edward seems to want to say something. He opens

his mouth, then says nothing. He shrugs and walks out of the room.

Carlo died on January twenty-seventh. The ground was frozen, not allowing burial. Tom, the man who attended to the grounds and the horses, built a bonfire in the back field. He and the other servants dragged Carlo by sled and pitched his huge bulk into the flames. Emily watched from the window as the flames flickered over and around the body like fiery mist and then bloomed madly, engulfing her dear companion.

She would take no other dog.

NINETEEN

1866 – 1868

Dare you see a Soul at the "White Heat"?
Then crouch within the door –
Red – is the Fire's common tint –
But when the vivid Ore

Has vanquished Flame's conditions –
It quivers from the Forge
Without a color, but the Light
Of unannointed Blaze –

Ten years of living with a soul at white heat had buckled the frame of Emily Dickinson's being as a blacksmith's forge buckles an iron rod.

The ten years from 1855 to 1865 were a decade of intimacy nurtured and destroyed, of hopes raised and crushed, of vision lost and regained, of health destroyed and partially recovered—and a decade of ecstatic, despairing poetry that was ripped from her soul as seeds are wrested from a pomegranate.

All set in motion by a love so big it left her faint and white.

At first the changes came slowly. When she was not making the morning bread or working in the garden, Emily remained for longer and longer periods of time in her bedroom. But she still came down to eat meals with Vinnie and Mother and Father. If she was downstairs, and visitors came to the door, she would still welcome them, but if she knew someone else was there to greet them, she glided up the back staircase to the safe refuge of her room. When a friend like the newspaper editor Samuel Bowles stopped by to say hello, she felt an impulse to run and hide . . . but for now, she fought the impulse, invited the friend into the front parlor, and sat and chatted with him. Yet she had changed in subtle ways. Her friends noticed that her breath was labored, and that—perhaps despite herself—she was waiting for them to leave.

The tensions of polite expectation still stretched her behavior on a familiar rack, but rips were beginning to show.

She began to dress more eccentrically. She favored a white pique accented with nothing more than a blue worsted shawl. Over time, white was becoming her main color, her only color. As with her behavior, the change was gradual. From time to time she still wore the calico and wool that she had been so fond of in the past. But more and more those articles of clothing remained hanging on a peg in her wardrobe.

At some level beneath words, she was answering Wadsworth's recriminating query, "Why didn't you come to me in white?"

As she withdrew, she started to inhabit her memories. She recalled and relived scenes from her childhood and her early adulthood. Though her blindness had dissipated, it had left her with an enhanced inner vision. As she revisited her memories now, they flashed with startling clarity, and the softer light of understanding transformed them into an experience that was all new.

In a way she was putting herself back together after the past decade had blasted her apart.

TWENTY

She remembered especially the hard times—they returned with a vengeance. The shame of losing the family Homestead. That night, during the tenth year of her life, when they all first found out that they would have to move.

Father occupies the head of the dinner table with the air of a monarch secure enough in his throne to be amiably disposed when he so chooses. He is oddly affable tonight, yet his eyes glitter with danger. His dark hair, already flecked with silver, is neatly cropped about his handsome face, and his shrewd remarks dominate the room. He greets his children one by one as they slide politely into their seats. To Austin, Father nods his head with mock obeisance and asks him a question about his studies, which Austin answers haltingly but well in his grainy, slightly husky voice. The boy has the air of someone who knows he must meet certain strict expectations, but also knows he will be granted indulgences because he is male.

As the girls take their seats, Father purses his lips in a comical expression to Vinnie and asks her if the day has met her youthful expectations, to which she replies in the affirmative, with a quick glance in the direction of Emily. For it is to Emily that Father turns his fullest attention, inquiring about her search for wildflowers and questioning her understanding of the Linnaean system of classifying them. His eyes linger on her face after she fully acquits herself of a thorough, detailed, and precise explanation. Then they turn to greet Emily's mother (also named Emily), who has just come in from the kitchen with the serving girl, bearing the steaming plate of roast lamb and potatoes.

Across the activity of the table and children, Father informs Mother about the details of the approaching move to West Street. Mother answers in subdued tones that suggest deference and respect, though from time to time, between words, her eyes flash with little bursts of meaning that only she and her husband understand.

During a pause, the man who is taking the house from them, General Mack, can be heard speaking behind the closed door that separates the East half of the house, where the Dickinsons currently live, from the West.

Vinnie asks, "Why did Grandfather lose this house?"

"Hush," Mother snaps.

"Let the child speak," Father intones in a soft voice that reminds Emily, for some reason, of a snake's flickering tongue. "What is it you say, girl? Speak up."

"I want to know why General Mack owns our house now, and why we've had to share it all these years, and why Grandfather let him have it, and why we now must move to West Street." Under the table Emily's foot nudges her, but Vinnie is undeterred. "I want to know why Grandfather let that happen." She turns her fearless gaze upon Father.

Mother's eyes grow round as she looks across the table towards her husband. But he seems to welcome the question.

"Let this be a lesson," he tells his children, and they all grow silent under the sudden incursion into his tone of steely Puritanism. His diction slows and elevates, as if to allow the room a moment to prepare itself to receive his pronouncement. "Let this be a lesson about how one should conduct his affairs in life, about prudence in financial matters, about never outspending one's means, and about hard work. Let the Dickinsons never forget that this day—this, perhaps our last day in our family homestead—is a day of disgrace in the history of our family. And a day from which we shall recover." He looks about the room, perhaps to see if anyone cares to disagree. His lips move as if he tastes ashes.

No one is eating. Even the servant girl stands frozen.

"But why did he let it happen?" Vinnie pursues, still unafraid.

"He didn't mean to," Mother intercedes. "Sometimes things just happen."

"Life is never just a 'happen,'" Father proclaims. "I do not want ever to hear any of you use that as an excuse. Bad things happen when people lose their will."

"What is a 'will?'" Vinnie asks.

"It is a legal document that sets forth who gets your things when you die," Austin replies, bravely sailing his boat into the eye of the conversation.

"Can't we find Grandfather's will for him?" Vinnie queries. "It might be in your office, Father. If we find it, maybe we can get the house back."

"He's not talking about that kind of will," Emily informs Vinnie quietly, almost as an aside. "He means the desire that people have to work for their highest goals in life."

Father's eyes gaze at his elder daughter. "That was well said, Emily. Sometimes I consider it a shame that the law is not open to women, for you have a mind well suited to its fine distinctions—more so than any other member of the fairer sex, at least in my experience."

Emily listens without answering.

"And tell me, do you have a will at this early age in your life?" he inquires with carefully calibrated condescension.

Emily pauses a moment before answering. "I should like to have all the possibilities open to me that are open to Austin."

"That, I am afraid, will never happen. Women are not suited to a life of public discourse," Father tells her.

"So say the men," she murmurs.

"With good reason," Father counters, piling some peas onto his fork. "Now perhaps you might let me know if you have any will relating to more obtainable goals?"

"I like to flatter myself that I do, Father," Emily replies, bowing her head.

"And what might they be?"

"To be good, Father."

"Look at me, child, as you speak."

"To be good, Father."

They meet: Father's cold, demanding, but not unkind blue eyes; his daughter's dark caramel eyes, so clear, so intelligent and so far-seeing. Two slabs of unyielding New England granite, equal in flintiness, but not in size.

✦

Emily recalled a second scene, five years later, when Father first announced his plan to regain the family Homestead. It came one evening as he took her out for a drive.

Emily settles herself beside her father as he takes the

reins, nods to the hired man, shakes his arms, and clucks twice to the horse. Edward is famous for owning the finest horse in Amherst, with a glossy chestnut coat, beautiful lines, and a strong, sinewy eagerness for speed.

They begin at a trot, turning left briskly onto West Street. Edward clucks again, then again, and briefly, lightly applies the whip. The horse is a natural pacer, and through training it has learned to stride as quickly as many horses gallop. Trees stream by them on either side, dark and lovely against the mild expanse of light in the evening sky. The street unrolls below them at a dizzying speed. The wheels whiz, the shoes clip crisply, the air smells of autumn leaves, distant smoke, and deliciously of horse. The horse's gait is perfect, the road is even and well tended. Edward leans forward, urging the creature on. "Isn't this grand!" he calls to his daughter.

They negotiate the intersection with Main Street and come flying onto Broadway and down the hill towards Amherst College. Some young scholars leap out of the way as they sail by. "It's that damn Squire Dickinson!" one of them is heard to say, cursing a rounder oath as they disappear into the night. Emily hides her face slightly; she is smiling in the dusk.

They take another left turn, then another, and now they are coming up Main Street. The former Dickinson homestead looms on their right, its windows lit for the night—the largest house on the street. Edward seems to pick up the pace as they approach it. "Ten more years!" he calls to Emily.

"Ten more years till when?" she asks.

"I have a plan!" he answers without answering.

They fly by the house and climb Main Street to the intersection with West Street. They turn right by the straw-works factory, turn right again, and rattle to a stop in the driveway as the first few stars begin to distill like jewels out of the twilit mist.

Edward is panting with excitement as he lifts Emily down from her seat and turns the chaise back to the hired man.

"Will you let me take him out sometime, Father? On my own?" She coughs.

"Have you lost your senses, girl?"

"I heard you tell Austin he will be riding on his own soon."

"Emily, do I need to explain the difference?"

"That I am but a girl?"

Father opens his mouth as if to answer, but he says nothing. He strides away, complete in his masculine pride.

"Father!"

He stops, amazed that she has called after him. He turns and looks toward her, without speaking.

"Father, *what* will happen in ten years?"

A pleased amusement plays over his face. "I will tell you, if you keep my secret."

"Of course I will keep your secret."

He raises himself to his full height. "The Homestead will be ours again. In ten years, Emily, it will be ours. As it should be." His right hand grips the air. "We will rise up from the ashes of our defeat and humiliation."

"But how?" she asks.

He smiles but doesn't answer.

"Can I help you in some way, Father, in this quest?"

He waves his hand and walks away. He is muttering to himself, the happy mutterings of a man who needn't explain himself to his daughter.

Now, in the reconsiderings of memory, it was all so clear: Society granted Father the power to define the family landscape, but granted her none. And so the granite of her being was pushed slowly underground. She did what she had to, to survive: She learned to hollow out secret mines and tunnels in her life, in her mind.

TWENTY-ONE

1866 – 1868

Emily remembered Susan Gilbert of long ago sitting in the garden in West Street, in the shade of the Evergreen copse that Austin planted. At nineteen they were still not too old to be discussing what kind of birds they would each be. Susan said she would be a raven; Emily had consigned herself to being a humble wren. The two girls sat with their backs against a tree, snuggling against each other as cozily as if they really were two little birds in a nest.

We have all seen these intense bonds between young women on the verge of adulthood—friendships that are perfect at the time and seem certain to last forever—only to be bent or broken outright as one of the friends is captured by the gravitational pull of a new and different force. Remembering her tender affection

for Susan then, Emily realized that she was doubly innocent at the time: of the change that was coming, and
of the unexpected proximity of Susan's new object of
attraction.

"Aren't we poetic, though," Susan remarks wryly.

"What a wonderful thing it is to be friends. Susie, I
want our friendship to never end."

Susan glances back towards the house. "Is Austin
up yet?"

"Oh, he went out on an errand." Emily leans closer
and confides, "I think he's mailing a letter to Mattie."

"That's nice of him. But not without pain."

Emily seems to miss the significance of Susan's last
statement. "Susie, some day you and I might be related—if Austin marries your sister Mattie. Won't that be
grand?"

"It would."

"I guess we wouldn't be sisters-in-law exactly, but
we would in a way. And I already feel like we're sisters.
Don't you feel somehow that we are sisters?"

At this point Susan stands and turns away. "Emily,
I'm going to tell you something now and I don't want
you to think worse of me for it. Although of course you
may if you wish."

"Why, Susie? I'm sure I would never think worse
of you."

"Just listen. Austin has asked me to go riding with him tonight. I'm going in private, of course." She smooths her hair behind her ear.

"I think it's nice of you to keep him company." Emily is looking down at the ground, rubbing a design into the dirt with a small stick.

"I'm not merely keeping him company."

The stick stops moving. "I don't understand," Emily says finally.

"Austin has shown some interest in me."

"I thought he liked Mattie."

"I can't speak for his feelings."

"Does Mattie know?" The stick has started to move slowly across the dirt.

"She is starting to realize."

Emily stands.

A carriage rolls up smartly, and Susan turns, pulls herself erect, and looks towards the carriage with an expectant smile. Emily sees that her friend's attention has been drawn off by a tidal pull of attraction.

But it isn't her brother, not this time. Edward Dickinson is driving the carriage, and his eyes glint with pleasure as he spots Susan Gilbert and his daughter. "May I offer you ladies a ride?" he barks, gesturing proudly to the empty seat beside him in the chaise.

"I would love to," Susan replies. "Sitting beside a man who really knows how to handle horses is thrilling."

"Well, now, I wouldn't go that far . . ." Edward mumbles happily.

"Don't deny your skill, sir. Taut reins and a head held high—it makes all the difference. There are so few who do it properly." The proud way Susan holds her own head brings out the beauty of her long white neck.

"I've found that to be true," Edward purrs. "Emily?"

"Not now," she replies.

"Oh, do come, Emily," Susan tells her. "Please. I wouldn't want to go without you."

"I'd like you to go."

Father looks back and forth between the two young women, a puzzled expression on his face. Whatever the interaction he has missed, it doesn't register as important in his world. "You're sure, Emily? It's a glorious day for a drive, and what man wouldn't want two such beautiful passengers?" he barks.

"One will do for now, Father."

Susan tips her head, eyebrow raised, but Emily shakes her head no. She turns back to her garden as Father hops out of the carriage and gallantly helps Susan up into her seat. Susan sparkles under the attention of the older man, and there is little doubt that she has found a conquest and a very willing future father-in-law.

With growing passion, Emily starts to cut the deadheads off the roses.

Later that evening, Emily is sitting at the stone hearth, letting her eyes wash over the fading orange of the coals in the fireplace. Her mind has reached the dull place before sleep.

The front door opens, a few loud, definite steps ring in the hallway, and a figure appears in the door. "Emily, is that you?"

"Yes, Austin. I don't know who else it might be." She shakes herself back from the edge of sleep.

"It might be Vinnie."

"You can't hear her snoring upstairs?"

"Emily, I've . . . I've brought someone to see you." And Austin steps into the room, leading Susan by his hand.

"Good evening, Emily," Susan says. She is smiling brightly, but something about her manner is hesitant.

"Good evening."

"Well . . . may we come sit with you?" Austin asks.

"Yes, of course."

Austin drags a few more chairs over to the hearth. He and Susan look at each other once or twice; their faces are flushed and excited.

"I say, we had a wonderful ride, didn't we, Susan?"

"We certainly did. I had two wonderful rides to-day." They exchange a smile.

"How sweet of Father to do that. Wasn't he sweet, Emily?"

"Yes, Austin. He was sweet," Emily says.

Austin smiles, and a confiding warmth comes into his voice. "I've told Susan all about the wonderful talks we've had here on the hearth. On this very spot."

Emily stands up. "Austin, if you would excuse me, I should like to go to bed."

Susan reaches across and takes her hand. "Please don't, Emily. I would be so very happy if you would stay up with us for a little."

"'Us?'"

"With Austin . . . and with me."

"I'm sorry, Susie. I really am tired."

"Please? Just for a moment? To give us some time— all three of us? Please, Emily—don't be heartless."

"Susie, you know me better than that."

"You mustn't think anything is changed between you and me," Susan says, still holding Emily by the hand. "In fact . . . the happiness I feel now is all the greater because you and I will be true sisters."

Emily squeezes Susan's hand, but avoids her eye.

They talk in low voices, laughing now and then, Austin and Susan doing most of the conversing. At ten Austin takes Susan home and Emily goes up to bed.

Looking back at the memory, Emily understood what she hadn't been able to grasp at the time. Each of them had wanted something that might have been possible but for the conflicting wishes of the others. Emily wanted Austin to continue to see the world through her eyes and she wanted Susan to be her closest confidant; Susan wanted to better her station in life by becoming a part of the Dickinson family and she was willing to take on Austin as the price she had to pay, but was not willing to love him; and Austin wanted Susan as the pretty prize who would submit to his desires and needs, while he still kept Emily as his confidant.

It was quite simply an impossible situation, and seeing it all in retrospect, it was easy to understand why both her friendship with Susan and Austin's marriage to her had been quietly strangled over the course of time.

Three ropes, tangled in hopeless knots.

TWENTY-TWO

1868 – 1874

Early in 1868 Emily received word that Wadsworth and his family were moving back to Philadelphia. He was returning partly for medical reasons: an unspecified throat problem was limiting his effectiveness in the pulpit by hindering his enunciation. Emily's first poem of that year left little doubt about the continuing strength of her feelings for him.

The smouldering embers blush –
Oh Heart within the Coal
Hast thou survived so many years?
The smouldering embers smile –

Soft stirs the news of Light
The stolid seconds glow
This requisite has Fire that lasts
It must at first be true –

It would be eight more years before she and Wadsworth began to exchange occasional letters through the Hollands, and twelve years before he visited her again, but having him back in the East brought her closer to "thy long Paradise of Light."

In 1868 Emily was doing the work of the household—a vast amount of labor that we, with our washing machines and dishwashers and other domestic machinery, can scarcely begin to appreciate.

There was still no serving girl in the house. Emily baked, cleaned dishes, cooked, washed clothes, and cared for her parents. She labored from dawn to dusk, taking only short breaks. Some of the work she enjoyed—the baking, the working in the garden—but much of it was duty, which she accepted without question. She helped with the growing family next door—her nephew and niece.

Constrained by her new level of domestic duties, Emily wrote only ten poems in 1866, twelve in 1867, and eleven in 1868. But even after Maggie, the new servant, finally joined the family in 1868, she would never equal the astonishing output of poetry she composed during the ferment and anguish of the early 1860's. As if still suffering from emotional exhaustion after the turbulence of her earlier years, she would never again write more than forty-eight poems in a single year. As she observed in 1861,

A wounded Deer – leaps highest –
I've heard the Hunter tell
'Tis but the extasy of death –
And then the Brake is still!

Her wound hadn't stilled her after her leap, but it had taken its toll.

She wrote frequent letters to her friends, in between her many chores, but otherwise, except for close family, her life now was solitary. She received no visitors but those who remained outside her bedroom, speaking from behind the door left ajar.

As Susan and Austin's children grew, Emily became a doting aunt—sending small presents to the Evergreens accompanied by exquisite notes or poems, greeting them secretly in the "Northwest Passage" in the back hall of the Homestead. She was becoming a local legend, an eccentric, a famous recluse.

She finds an innocent pleasure in staging childlike pranks for the benefit of her nephew Ned and her niece Mattie and their playmates. She leaves cookies and treats in out-of-the-way places and writes cryptic clues as to their whereabouts. Once, when Ned leaves his overcoat in the Homestead, she returns it to the Evergreens with a card on one pocket that says "Come in" and a card on the other pocket that says "Knock." The first pocket contains raisins, and the second, some nuts.

The local children who play with Ned and Mattie are accustomed to the strange ways of the Dickinsons, Amherst's leading family. First of all, at the Evergreens, there is Austin, the father, who wears bright yellow suits, yells at the children from time to time, and is often seen racing about town in the finest horse and carriage in town. Then, the mother, Susan, is rather distant and distracted and severe, and always seems to be busy making plans for her dinner parties. At the Homestead, the grandparents are quiet and private people who seem astounded by the sight of children when Mattie or Ned brings a friend over. The one aunt, Lavinia (or Vinnie), is a proud, stiff woman who tends to lower her dignity long enough only to make inappropriate remarks about the children's parents. Whenever Mattie has a squabble with a friend, the children all know that Lavinia will come blustering out of nowhere and accost the child. "Your mother was just as false to her playmates as you are. It runs in your blood," she will say. Or "I knew your mother when she was every bit as pigeon-toed and pigeon-brained as you appear to be."

And then there is the other aunt no one ever sees, Emily. Mattie and Ned swear they see her and talk to her—in fact, they claim she is their strongest supporter when they get in trouble with their parents—but no one else ever catches a glimpse.

One day early in June, 1872, as the children play tag among the large trees outside the Homestead, a squarish old basket appears in the sky above them. It is being lowered by a rope from an upstairs window. One of the children stops and points. The others leave off the game and press around Ned and Mattie.

"What's in it?" they ask Ned, who is nearly eleven and knows most things.

He turns his large brown eyes skyward. "I have no idea."

"I see someone behind the window!" one of the children cries.

"That's Aunt Emily's room!" Mattie exclaims. "What is she doing?"

Down the basket plunges, closer and closer, swaying a bit in the June breeze. It is a simple basket with a hinged top and a stout handle.

"Can you reach it?" one of the little ones asks Ned.

"Not yet," he says. He is a pale child, not confident, popular only with younger children.

"I bet there's something really good in there," the youngest girl announces.

"Like what?" her older brother asks.

"Like apples," she says.

"Apples aren't ripe yet," her brother tells her.

"I don't care."

Down it comes, falling to the level of Ned's shoulder, where it dangles in mid-air. He lifts the basket and unties the simple slipknot. The rope withdraws with a jerk then slithers back through the window.

Ned sets the basket on the ground and opens the top. There is something inside, wrapped in kitchen towels. He pulls back a towel and gives a cheer. "It's Aunt Emily's gingerbread!"

The chorus of children explodes in praise of Aunt Emily. A wraith in a simple white housedress stirs softly behind the window and is gone.

Emily's parents still lived in the house, but they were showing signs of advanced age. In 1872, Edward Dickinson resigned as treasurer of Amherst College because of his worsening health. He had become pale and weak, and Emily wrote to a friend that his appearance filled her with terror. In May of 1873—as the fear of death overcame his crusty old Yankee independence— Edward gave himself to God and accepted Jesus. Now Emily was the only member of the family who had not been formally saved.

Also in 1873, under pressure from business associates, Edward allowed himself to be elected to the state House of Representatives to lobby for Amherst's interests. He spent some of 1874 in Boston, but was forced to return home frequently because of a continuing illness that he claimed was merely a bout of chronic indigestion.

At the end of the June recess, Edward spends his last Sunday home with his daughter Emily, sitting in the garden. For more than an hour they don't speak. She is reading *Middlemarch* for the third time, savoring George Eliot's resplendent figures of speech in the opening section of the book, when Dorothea and her sister feast their eyes on the pool of light within the very gemstone that will later prove an image of the sisters' differences.

She reads aloud to her father a passage which describes a spider web as a symbol for the young women's entrapment in their social roles—and then asks why that injustice could not be balled up into nothing, like squashed cobweb, and thrown away.

"Who is this George Eliot? His commentary suggests he is a brilliant man," her father comments.

She does not tell Father that "he" is really a brilliant woman; she knows Father is ill, and she will not disturb his rest.

"How in the world have you made this garden so lovely?" Father asks after a while. It is the closest he has ever come in this life to giving her a compliment.

"Mother has taught me about flowers, and I picked up the rest through books and on my own," she answers blandly.

"Mother doesn't know all this. Look at the variety of plants, and the colors, and how glorious it all looks together. This is a work of art." His voice sounds much older now; it has the nasal whine of an old man, and her heart contracts with fear and love.

"We all take what is given and do with it what we may," she answers.

"I was proud to get this house back for the family. This Homestead. I never forgave my father for losing it."

"It does our souls better to forgive, I think."

"I suppose I should, now that I have been saved."

"Father, you have always been stubborn, you know."

"There is only one person in the world more stubborn than I."

She smiles. "And who is that?"

He raises an eyebrow toward her.

She looks out over the garden in stunned silence. She didn't think he'd noticed.

"It is nice of you to stay with me. You keep so often to yourself," he remarks.

She doesn't answer. She knows if she tries to respond, she will cry. Her father has never spoken to her like this before. She opens her book again and re-enters the glory of George Eliot's prose.

As shadows stretch their fingers across the lawn and the sun begins to set behind them, behind the Evergreens, he comments, "I would like it not to end."

Uneasy and embarrassed, she suggests that he might like to go for a walk with Austin.

A day later, back in Boston for the new legislative session, Father has a stroke and dies instantly. Emily does not attend the funeral service held in the entrance hall of the Homestead. She remains in her room and listens from behind a door left slightly ajar. She is consumed by tears. Her fierce New England stoicism is no more.

She writes to her cousins Louise and Frances Norcross,

Father does not live with us now – he lives in a new house. Though it was built in an hour it is better than this. He hasn't any garden because he moved after gardens were made, so we take him the best flowers, and if we only knew he knew, perhaps we could stop crying . . .

I cannot write any more, dears. Though it is many nights, my mind never comes home.

To another acquaintance she writes, *"His Heart was pure and terrible and I think no other like it exists."*

And the other man with a pure heart—the smouldering heart within the coal—will she ever see him again?

TWENTY-THREE

1880 – 1886

In 1880 Emily is almost fifty years old. She wears each day the same simple white housedress. She maintains her slim, childlike figure, her smooth skin, and her red hair swept in a brown silk net, with a brown silk tassel behind each ear. Her voice has become breathless with age and her heart has begun to beat irregularly. A doctor who pays house calls has noticed a strange, hollow sound in the offbeat of her heart. Occasionally for no apparent reason, she has a fainting spell. Other than that, she shows no sign of the pox. She has been spared the ravages of skin lesions and open boils.

By summer of 1880, running water has been installed in the Homestead, partly to ease Mother's care. Mother has survived a major stroke and now lives, an invalid, in the bedroom behind Emily's, and Vinnie and Emily take turns caring for her. Vinnie is still shielding her older sister: a year earlier, on July fourth, when a great fire in Amherst drew Emily out of bed and generated so much light that Emily could see "a caterpillar measure a leaf far down in the orchard," Vinnie told her it was "only the fourth of July." Emily played along with her protector. As she wrote to the Norcrosses, "I thought if she felt it best to deceive, it must be that it was . . . I think she will tell us so when we die, to keep us from being afraid."

The family interactions, never simple, have woven themselves into a hopeless tangle. Austin never misses a chance to complain to Emily about his wife Susan. "She is heartless. Every new minute brings an improved cruelty," he declares, his eyes bulging with fury. "Not to mention the money that she and my spendthrift daughter waste—on jewels, dresses, and their precious dinner parties! Dancing until all hours of the night! It's becoming impossible to live there! What's a man to do?"

Emily does not reply; she knows too well the value of silence.

In two years Austin will begin an open relationship with Mabel Loomis Todd, a woman almost thirty years younger than he, the wife of an instructor of astronomy at Amherst College. As a gesture of friendship in 1882, Mabel sends Emily a painting of some Indian pipes, and Emily writes back, "That without suspecting it you should send me the preferred flower of life, seems al-

most supernatural." In return, she sends Mabel a poem
about a hummingbird.

> *A Route of Evanescence*
> *With a revolving Wheel –*
> *A Resonance of Emerald*
> *A Rush of Cochineal –*
> *And every Blossom on the Bush*
> *Adjusts it's tumbled Head –*
> *The Mail from Tunis – probably,*
> *An easy Morning's Ride –*

Austin's relationship with Mabel will last until the
end of his life.

The recluse Emily Dickinson is known in town
for the witty, elegant notes of decline that she sends
to would-be visitors. To Maria Whitney, who comes
calling, she writes, *"How precious to hear you ring at the
door, and Vinnie ushering you to those melodious moments
of which friends are composed . . . Remembrance is the great
tempter."* She still feels the debts of affection but cannot
bear to discharge them in person.

In the past fifteen years, only a handful of people
outside her immediate family have seen her face-to-
face: two children who sang for her once; a delivery
boy who caught her by surprise; the newspaper editor Samuel Bowles, who called up to her, "Emily, come
down here, you damned rascal," when she at first

refused to see him; and the editor Thomas Higginson, who visited her twice, complained that she drained his nerve power, and declined to publish her unorthodox poetry.

Only occasionally does Emily hint at the bandaged secret of love and illness that she, with Wadsworth, has been keeping. In a poem to an old friend, she explains why she cannot tell anyone

> For what I shunned them so –
> Divulging it would rest my Heart
> But it would ravage theirs.

She will keep her secret.

But four years earlier, in 1876, Emily and Wadsworth had begun to exchange letters again through the Hollands. She recorded her reaction in a poem that year:

> Long Years apart – can make no
> Breach a second cannot fill –
> The absence of the Witch does not
> Invalidate the spell –
>
> The embers of a Thousand Years
> Uncovered by the Hand
> That fondled them when they were Fire
> Will stir and understand.

During the four years of their renewed correspondence, he has never once mentioned what he is about to do.

It is a mild and lovely evening in Amherst. Emily is tending her lilies and heliotropes in the garden behind and to the East of the Homestead. At the height of summer in 1880—at summer's full—the grounds have never looked more beautiful. Lilies tip forward, giving their yellow and orange angular faces to the caress of the fading sun; heliotropes bloom purplish blue in tiny, fragrant clusters of sun-seeking desire. Emily is bending down to weed the bed when she sees Vinnie running toward her, waving her hand. Though Vinnie has put on some weight over the years, she is still strong and athletic, and she runs quickly.

Emily's heart contracts. Perhaps Mother has failed. She stands and watches as her sister comes closer.

"What is it?" she croaks.

"He is here," Vinnie pants out, coming to a stop.

"Who is here?" Emily asks, brushing away a fly. She does not allow her relief to show: Vinnie always tells her that she thinks, and worries, too much.

"I heard him ask Maggie if you were in," Vinnie pants.

"Vinnie, you know I do not accept visitors."

"The gentleman with the deep voice wants to see you, Emily."

Emily turns and looks towards the house. "*He* is here?" she says.

Vinnie nods.

"He gave me no warning."

"At least that's one thing he hasn't given you."

Emily raises her hands toward the heavens. "I will receive him, of course."

Vinnie frowns.

Wadsworth is standing in the front entryway when she glides in to greet him from the back hallway, a slim flame of white against the darkness. She sees right away that he has aged greatly. Standing seems to pain him and he is leaning on an elegantly carved wooden cane. His jowls have grown in bulk to the point that they tug down the sides of his mouth giving his face an expression of glum disappointment. Two deep canyons descend at an angle from either side of his nose, cutting into the flesh of his cheeks. His right cheek especially looks more scarred, as if he has had recent skin problems. Though his golden-brown eyes still peer at her with the concentrated force of his brilliant and graceful intellect, the eyeballs have a yellowish cast. He has lost all the hair on top of his head, and jagged lines are etched into his forehead like a system of river tributaries. His skin is pale and gray.

"Good evening, Master," she says. She is aware of a great stillness around them; the world has stopped turning and the stars are giving thought as to whether they will come out tonight.

"Good evening, Daisy," he replies.

"Where did you come from?" she asks, thinking that he looks and sounds like an apparition. "And why did you not tell me you were coming, so I could have it to hope for?"

"Because I did not know it myself. I stepped from my pulpit to the train."

"How long did it take?"

"Twenty years," he tells her, with inscrutable roguery.

"Now I know it is really you," she says laughing, and she steps in closer to him. They take each other's hand. His hand is still gentle and strong. "Welcome back, my Philadelphia."

"Your Philadelphia has grown older," he says.

"As all things must. But that does not lessen them," she replies. "It only reminds us of their majesty." She feels the tears coming and blinks them back.

"You have hardly changed at all," he says. "You look as young and beautiful as I remember."

"I have never been the recipient of one of those adjectives, and the other thankfully, I left long ago," she says, turning so that he can't see her emerging tears.

"And yet you look exactly as I remember you."

"I have changed in all ways that matter," she replies. She steps away from him and enters the front parlor knowing that he will follow. She approaches the window and gazes out across the street. Now that it is August, rounded mounds of cut hay dot the surface of the meadow casting long blue-gray shadows towards the east. She envisions two figures, a man and a woman picking their way between the haycocks, on their way to some timeless meeting in the swamp and the distant woods.

"How do you mean?" he asks, coming up beside her.

She continues to look out the window as she talks. "I was but a girl when I saw you last. Now I am a woman. Most people grow up over many years, starting when they are young. I grew up late, and very fast."

"I am sorry for the role I played," he says softly.

"I will not deny the pain I felt, nor will I deny how necessary it was. There can be no summer without the heaves of storm that chase off winter."

"The theory of antagonisms."

"Yes," she replies, smiling slightly. "The acorn finally took root, not without some help."

He places a hand, trembling slightly, on her arm. "The affliction you hinted at in one of your letters . . . It has struck me over the years as horrific and unfair, for you had no way of knowing . . ." He lets his voice trail off.

"Do you think I didn't know beforehand?" she asks, turning and looking into his eyes. Her eyes, darker than sherry, are brimming with tears.

"I don't understand," he says. His face seems younger now, as he peers back at her—his pupils contract with a shift of light within or without. For a moment he is the young man she met twenty-five years ago.

"Do you think I didn't understand why your children were so many years in arriving, and why your hands always seemed to be covered with painful sores?" she asks.

He takes her hand. "I don't know whether to be more grieved or less," he tells her.

"There is no need for either." They exchange another look. As if dazed he drops her hand, steps back and rests his weight against his cane.

"I am sorry to keep you standing. Would you like to have a seat on the sofa while I get something to eat or drink? We have some graham bread, freshly baked, New England style," she says, with a little lilt in her voice.

"Yes, thank you. And then I must be going. My coach awaits me outside."

"You are staying with Charles Clark tonight?"

"Yes, in Northampton."

She disappears into the kitchen and returns a few minutes later with some graham bread and some currant wine, both of which she has made herself. She takes a seat beside him and serves him, and they eat and drink in silence, almost like an old married couple who have no more secrets and no need to discuss anything. It is clear from the way he eats that he finds the bread delicious.

After many minutes of silence she asks after his children. He explains that his oldest child, Charles Jr., showed a streak of rashness a few years earlier and left the religion so precious to him. Recently there have been signs that he might return—in fact he has mentioned the possibility of wanting to enter the ministry. His daughter Edith has run off from the family with a much older man, and they have not heard from her in over a year. And then there is the youngest, Willie.

"And what is Willie like?" Emily asks. She can see the humor creeping back into his face, like children converging on a forbidden treat as their parents nod off to sleep.

"He reminds me of you."

"Of me? What do you mean?" she asks.

"He is a pure soul, unblemished by the world."

"How so?"

He brushes a crumb from his lip. "Should he find a gold watch in the street, he would not pick it up, so unsullied is he."

"You love him very much."

"I love them all very much. But the oldest two have already broken my heart."

"And they will repair it as they grow up."

He finishes off the currant wine. "That was excellent."

"Thank you."

He turns and looks at her. "I am liable at any time to die."

The news has struck her almost dumb; she would like to say something, but cannot.

"The affliction has eaten away at me. I am weak and old—old beyond my years."

"Your spirit and intelligence are still strong," she manages to say.

He looks out the window at the fading light. "I needed to come here to take leave of you," he tells her.

"I have never had a more glad surprise."

He places his hand on hers. "And now I must go."

She sighs and pats his hand.

Again they are saying good-bye outside the front door. Again they are faces on two decks, on ships bound for separate shores.

He looks off into the distance, tilting his head slightly to the side, as if listening to something.

"Frogs?" he asks.

"Yes. They are out in the swamp."

They both listen to the far-off musical cry. She is picturing the yellow violets, so far away in the night.

"Frogs are my Willie's little friends," he tells her.

"They are my dogs," she replies.

He gives her his last smile. "I looked over the flowers recently, and they spoke at quite a volume," he says.

"I am glad." She is looking up at him, trying to fix the golden-brown glow of his eyes forever in her mind.

"But you already know you have become great."

She doesn't answer; it is her form of assent.

They say good-bye without words. They take each other's hands. As he leaves, she offers him a daisy. He walks off into the twilight, resting his weight against his cane.

TWENTY-FOUR

On April 1, 1882, the Reverend Charles Wadsworth died in Philadelphia.

Half a year later, in November of 1882, Mother also died. In that year of partings, her death also followed a meeting, a reconciliation of sorts as Emily discovered a new and unexpected closeness with her mother while caring for her in her final months. After Mother's death Emily wrote to her friend Mrs. Holland, *"We were never intimate Mother and Children while she was our Mother – but Mines in the same Ground meet by tunneling and when she became our Child, the Affection came."*

The events of the past few years had somehow freed Emily Dickinson, and at the age of fifty-one she conducted a spirited epistolary romance with Otis Lord, an old and distinguished judge, a friend of her father's whose wife had recently passed away. In a letter on April 30, 1882 she confided her loss to him:

"My Philadelphia has passed from the Earth . . . Which Earth are we in?"

Over the years, Emily had seen Otis Lord from time to time, and now he asked to be allowed to visit her, but she requested instead that they keep in touch by letter. Declining his offer of marriage, she wrote to him, "Don't you know that 'No' is the wildest word we consign to Language?" She proposed that they write to each other each Sunday. For a few years until his death they shared their love of Shakespeare and high literary jokes. She had found a balance of affection and solitude that suited her.

❧

In October, 1883, Austin's and Susan's youngest child Gib develops a sudden fever and hovers near death. He is only eight years old. He is Austin's pride, a very popular boy about town with both children and adults, full of a remarkable spirit and intelligence that strike everyone who knows him. For several years he has been Emily's favorite.

As he weakens on the night of October 13, Emily makes her way over to the Evergreens. It is the first time she has entered Susan's and Austin's home in more than fifteen years. She stands vigil at Gib's bedside, but the odor of disinfectants apparently sickens her; she faints and is brought back to the Homestead. Gib dies later that night of complications from typhoid fever.

For weeks afterwards, Vinnie and Emily fear for Austin's life. He has taken to bed and seems to have lost the will to live. Though moving about and walking, Susan too is stricken. Casting off the distance that has separated them, Emily writes Susan one of her most touching prose passages, an elegy for her nephew:

No crescent was this Creature – He traveled from the Full –

Such soar, but never set –

I see him in the Star, and meet his sweet velocity in everything that flies – his Life was like the Bugle, which winds itself away, his Elegy an echo – his Requiem ecstasy –

Dawn and Meridian in one.

Although Austin recovers his health, Emily does not. She begins to suffer frequent fainting spells, and her heartbeat grows more irregular. Again the family physician notes that strange hollowness in the offbeat. It never occurs to him to attribute it to the heart's destruction by the pox.

In June of 1884, Emily is making a cake with Maggie when she sees a great darkness coming and faints. She is unconscious until late that night and stays in bed for weeks. She suffers similar spells of fainting and weakness through 1885 and into the spring of 1886.

Over the past few years she has written many letters to Wadsworth's old friend James Clark, and after

James' death, to his brother Charles. Now, in April of 1886, Emily sends him one of the last letters she will ever write. She recounts the story of Wadsworth's last visit to her and she quotes the ending to one of his most famous sermons, "Going Home." It is a sermon about seeking redemption in the peace and glory of the heavens. She adds, *Was he not an Aborigine of the sky?"*

TWENTY-FIVE

On the morning of May 13, 1886, Emily Dickinson feels faint and loses consciousness. She remains unconscious through a day and a half of heavy, labored breathing. Finally, just before 6:00 in the evening on May 15, with Vinnie at her side and Austin nearby, she dies. She is folded in a little white wrap that her cousin, Clara Newman Turner, has sewn for her. Following Emily's orders, the service is simple, and when it ends, the Dickinson's six hired men lift her casket on their shoulders and carry her—not out the front door, for all to see—but down the back hall and through the Northwest Passage and out. They bear her across three fields, past her favorite nodding daisies and the humming bees, to her simple resting place in the cemetery.

Before the coffin is closed Vinnie places two fragrant purple flowers by Emily's hand. She says they are "to take to Judge Lord," but she is protecting her sister one last time. They are heliotropes—seekers of the sun. They are to help Daisy find her sun; they are for Charles Wadsworth.

Later, Vinnie will tell people that Emily's withdrawal from the world had no real cause—it was only a "happen." To the very end, she is her big sister's protector.

But Vinnie's big sister has never really needed a protector. In her long, solitary journey Emily Dickinson taught herself well how to find her way home through darkness.

In the stillness of the sleeping house, at some unearthly hour that is neither midnight nor dawn, a wraith in white starts down the stairs to the kitchen one last time, in her own, greater silence. The glow of the candle conjures a halo of soft brilliance about her moving figure; wall and banister and tread take shape around her with an intimacy that she remembers like a tingle through her skin. She enters the kitchen, and across the room, beyond the throw of her flame, drawers and cabinets have already begun to etch their solid, familiar outlines in the silvergray twilight. Her glass measuring cup and silver spoon glint with a faint, rosy light.

Outside, a visitor is coming down the walk. She spies him through the window and watches him approach. He glances about restlessly; he is waiting for someone.

She pulls open the door and floats out into the shimmering morning. The silver dome of heaven is tolling like a bell. As she looks toward the visitor, her eyes are full of beauty and shadow. She is ready. Her last flight, like all her flights, will be in the company of what is most humble and most familiar, yet still most strange.

And he unrolled his feathers,
And rowed him softer Home –

Than Oars divide the Ocean,
Too silver for a seam,
Or Butterflies, off Banks of Noon,
Leap, plashless as they swim.

AFTERWORD

by William Norcross

A PLAUSIBLE LITERARY CONCEIT

As a medical doctor, I know that when a patient presents a variety of seemingly unrelated symptoms, it is best practice to look for one cause that accounts for them all. As I began to write this novel about Emily Dickinson, I found myself facing a similar situation. There were three great facts of Emily Dickinson's life that should be explained: her passionate and agonized love poems of the early 1860's, the partial blindness for which she sought treatment in Cambridge, Massachusetts during much of 1864 and 1865, and her subsequent withdrawal from the world after her return to Amherst. As I discovered her papers, and others' opinions of her and her poetry, I began to suspect that the most plausible explanation for all three facts was the new and probably controversial theory advanced in this novel that she, in fact, contracted syphilis from a love relationship with a married man, a minister—the much-admired Reverend Charles Wadsworth.

All theories aside, my main goal in writing this book was to honor an Emily Dickinson who possessed the intellectual rigor, the naïveté, the eccentricity, the passion, the despair, and the sly humor that we know and love from her poetry. It was also an irresistible challenge to try to create the dynamics of an all-encompassing emotional and intellectual relationship with a man whom she may have seen only four or five times in her life. It became pure joy to immerse myself in the poems and letters of perhaps our greatest American writer and try to infer the life from which they might have sprung.

Approaching Emily Dickinson's story as someone who loved her poetry, I sought first of all to understand as much as possible the circumstances behind its brilliant condensation. How did she evolve so quickly from the airy, discursive letter writing of her late adolescence to the focused, dense crystallizations of her mature poetry only a few years later? The more I read her love poetry, and the more I researched her life, the more I became convinced that the poems must refer to a real relationship with another human being—that the poems and the "Master" letters were not, as some critics once maintained, merely a pose or a mask or a

literary exercise. Even if the love was platonic or un-
requited, there must have been a beloved. Like many
biographers, I was left with the impression that the
experience gave her an emotional shock that not only
transformed her as a poet, *but also changed her life forever.*

There have long been whispers about "a lover" and
his or her identity, but the reports have been stained by
the enmity, the rumors, and the spin doctoring which
began surprisingly soon after Emily's death in 1886.
Here is a brief history. The problems began as Emily's
sister, Vinnie, tried to publish some of the hundreds
of poems that she discovered at Emily's death. She
sought aid from her sister-in-law Susan, who rebuffed
her. Perhaps Susan felt the poems were not worthy
of publication, or perhaps she feared the exposure of
her own marital discord or of Emily's deepest secrets
that she was not ready to reveal to the public. Vinnie
then turned for help to Mabel Loomis Todd, the young
married woman who was the (rather shockingly) open
mistress of their brother Austin. Austin was of course
Susan's husband and the older brother of Emily and
Vinnie. Once Mabel began to compile a collection of
poetry, Susan (living very unhappily still with Austin)
changed her mind and decided to publish her own col-
lections of Emily Dickinson's poems and letters, con-
sisting largely of the verses and notes that Emily had
sent to her over the years. Susan's daughter Martha

Dickinson Bianchi—Emily's niece—assisted her mother in this endeavor. Thus the publication of Emily Dickinson's poetry commenced under the competing banners of bitter intra-familial strife.

Trying to make her editions look more complete and authoritative, Martha smoothed over the long gaps and tortured strains in the relationship between Susan and Emily by *changing the dates of a number of the letters that Emily had sent to Susan.* Over the years, she proved herself to be highly unreliable in her claims of a lifelong closeness between her mother and her now-famous aunt.

Given this background, it should not surprise us that her most scandalous disclosure about her aunt was greeted with outright skepticism: the disclosure of Emily's secret love for a married man.

In 1924, Martha made the bold claim that Emily "met [her] fate" on a visit to Philadelphia—a clear reference to Charles Wadsworth. Her story of a love renounced to avoid "the inevitable destruction of another woman's life" was widely dismissed as sensationalism. Martha's subsequent efforts in 1932 to back up her contention that Emily had revealed her secret to Susan, Vinnie, Austin and others, were also met with derision.

The irony may be, however, that in this one instance she was telling the truth.

It is difficult to read Emily Dickinson today without concluding that her relationship—whether platonic or spiritual/physical—with "my dearest earthly friend" Wadsworth was a clear and central feature of her emotional life. The references to Philadelphia, to Master, to Saxon are consistent and persuasive, as are the letters to the Clarks after Wadsworth's death, as are the echoes between her poetry and Wadsworth's sermons, pointed out so brilliantly by biographers Richard Sewall and Alfred Habegger.

But does this mean that she must have contracted syphilis from Wadsworth, as the novel contends?

Obviously, I am of that opinion. To be fair, my theory is based on circumstantial evidence, and that evidence might look inconclusive in its separate pieces. But I would argue that it is rather suggestive taken as a whole. Here are some of the possible clues: Emily did have a serious vision disorder in 1864 and 1865, probably what we now call iritis or anterior uveitis—a major cause of which is syphilis and/or the auto-immune reactions which accompany syphilis—and the timing would suggest an initial infection sometime in 1860 or 1861; Wadsworth did visit the Dickinson homestead at least once in 1860 and again in 1880; Emily wrote in a letter that Wadsworth told her of "dark secrets" in his life; years earlier he was expelled from Hamilton College for an unauthorized absence, which could have been a sign of a turbulent youth; he complained in a letter of boils on his hands and he was afflicted with rheumatism, both of which can be symptoms of syphilis; his career was at times threatened by a voice ailment strikingly similar to an ailment caused by gonorrhea, which was often a fellow traveler of syphilis (Wadsworth left the Calvary Church in San Francisco earlier than expected either because of exhaustion or because of a voice ailment for which he sought treatment soon after his return to Philadelphia.); Wadsworth and his wife Jane were married for twelve years before the birth of their first child—a hint that perhaps there were miscarriages or stillbirths caused by the transfer of syphilis to her before the disease entered the latent stage and allowed for healthy birth; in her later years Emily had a breathless voice and an air of nervous exhaustion, conditions that were present in some other sufferers of syphilis; Emily apparently died of an undiagnosed heart ailment that was consistent with the ravages of cardiovascular tertiary syphilis—one of the three forms of advanced syphilis—which would mean the disease attacked her heart and not her skin. All those around Emily, including her closest relatives and friends, were extremely protective of her, in some cases destroying most or all of her correspondence—a level of secrecy that argues the existence of a secret.

Another fact is also significant: All of Emily Dickinson's letters to Wadsworth (with the exception of her drafts of the Master letters, which bear merely the salutation "Master") were destroyed at or before her death, and all of his letters to her were likewise consigned to oblivion. Out of the roughly one hundred friends and acquaintances with whom she exchanged letters, only with Wadsworth was such a total blanket of secrecy enforced; it seems that those letters were too dangerous to preserve. One might ask, why then did the Master letters survive? My hunch is that Emily simply could not bear to part with those letters, because they marked the three crucial stages of her love for Wadsworth: the ecstatic infatuation of the first letter, the agonized imploring of the second, and the crashing despair of the third.

Similarly, I would argue, Emily saved the one short note from Wadsworth not because it was an early expression of his interest in her, as is commonly supposed, but because it was the one written acknowledgement from Wadsworth of her "affliction," syphilis.

Because the theory is speculative, I would suggest that its appearance in this book constitutes a literary conceit—but a plausible conceit, and one that may offer more insight into Emily's life after 1863 than other explanations such as a social phobia or the after-effects of having been raised by an overbearing father. The theories do not need to be mutually exclusive: It is possible to argue that the contraction of syphilis could have intensified a pre-existing impulse towards solitude as a result of a social phobia and/or an over-protective upbringing. It seems likely, in fact, that more than one factor was necessary to bring about such an extreme level of withdrawal.

On a related and somewhat contentious issue, what about the identification of Charles Wadsworth as the "Master"?

There are those scholars today who believe that Susan was, in fact, the love of Emily's life, and that Emily Dickinson's poems of loss and pain refer to Susan. Perhaps. But now that scholars have finally established an accurate dating and sequence, the landscape of a sudden rupture in their relationship seems fairly clear, as is the fact that they pursued largely separate lives while living next door to one another. It was, in fact, the very opposite of the situation with the "Master," who apparently lived outside New England: Emily wrote to him, "Could you come to New England – this summer – would you come to Amherst – Would you like to come – Master?"

The biographer Alfred Habegger has argued that there are simply too many later references to the lover as a man, and as someone who lived outside of New England, and as someone whom Emily could contact only by letter, for Susan to be that love of her life. At the risk of taking issue with some critics and scholars who are at work today, I find his analysis persuasive. Certainly Susan was a love of Emily Dickinson's life, at least early on, and certainly the border between being a friend and a lover can be hazy. We can only speculate about the details of her relationship, whatever it may have been with Emily Dickinson.

While a biography can and must weigh different theories about what might have happened to its subject, a novel creates one view of a life and follows it to its logical conclusion. An historian has to be circumspect and judicious; a novelist can go right for the heart. In writing this novel I have tried nonetheless, to remain true to what is in the historical record. *I have invented no writing by Emily Dickinson or any of the principals.* I have also tried to be faithful to the currently accepted sequence and details of Emily Dickinson's life, while introducing in fictional form a speculative theory about her withdrawal from society.

Many of the scenes in the novel are built from small hints in the letters of Emily Dickinson or others. Emily's last afternoon with her father, for instance, is based on a letter she wrote to Thomas Higginson. The final scene with Wadsworth in 1880 is based on a letter she sent in 1886, after Wadsworth's death, to his friend Charles Clark. In that letter Emily mentions not only Wadsworth's statement about stepping from the pulpit to the train and his joke about its taking twenty years, but also his fond claim about Willie and the frogs, and the "last smile he gave me" when she replied that they were her dogs.

Other scenes in the novel are built on reasonable supposition based on available information. For example, we know from the diary of Eudocia Flynt that Emily and Vinnie did visit the Colemans in Middletown,

Connecticut on October 19, 1860.

I have drawn much of my understanding of the details and shape of Dickinson's life from two extraordinary and invaluable biographies, *The Life of Emily Dickinson*, by Richard B. Sewall, and *My Wars are Laid Away in Books*, by Alfred Habegger. (Richard Sewall, of course, is the first great Dickinson scholar, a figure of towering strength and importance.) Many recent pieces of feminist criticism, beginning with the landmark 1975 article, "The Female World of Love and Ritual," by Carroll Smith-Rosenberg, also enriched my understanding of Dickinson's life. I have sharpened my interpretation of Dickinson's poetry through my readings of, and disagreements with, the two insightful literary critics, Cynthia Griffin Wolff and Sharon Cameron. For information about Rye and Indian bread and Graham bread, I turned to recipe books and also to the charming pamphlet, "Emily Dickinson: Profile of the Poet as Cook," by Guides at the Dickinson Homestead. I am also thankful to Joe Beyer of the Calvary Presbyterian Church in San Francisco for his kindness in allowing access to the trustees' notes during research into Wadsworth's time in San Francisco.

❧

So ends my uncle William's manuscript. May I suggest that a glass of wine and a loaf of home-baked bread (no more than ½ gill of lard!) might be a fitting way to bid farewell?

Sincerely,

James Sulzer,
Nephew and Executor

ACKNOWLEDGMENTS

I owe my greatest debt to the readers who have encouraged me and given me guidance not only in this, but in other projects over the years. They are, first of all, my wife Barbara Elder, whose candor and judgment are unmatched; my friends Jamie McEwan and Joe Blatt, who never cease to give me invaluable and generous feedback; Joyce Engelson, who reviewed early drafts of the novel; Tom Congdon, who taught me more than anyone how to be a better writer; my friends Kathy Butterworth and Karen Borchert, who always give me highly informed judgment; and my brothers Mike and Steve, eternally gracious.

I want to thank Karetta Hubbard of Fuze Publishing for her faith in this book and for choosing to bring it to the world. She also helped me find and avoid countless dead ends of context and speculation in an earlier draft.

Special thanks also go out to the talented writer and editor, Sarah Pleydell, who edited the final version and helped me craft the ultimate shape of the manuscript. She was the editor every writer dreams about: a sympathetic reader who uses a tender touch to work wonders. Thanks also to Molly Best Tinsley for her excellent editorial guidance and suggestions, and to Ray Rhamey for his expert cover and book design.

I wrote this manuscript in an old garage out behind the house, surrounded by tools I had recently hung up on pegboard to clear out space for a small white desk; the significance of its color (and the white iBook I used) didn't occur to me until months after I completed the first draft! The rough cement floor was made cozier by the worn rug one of our sons gave to me as he graduated from his college apartment—a small example of the many ways our three children, Will, Rob and Kate, supported me through the frustrations and minor triumphs of the writing of this book. Keeping me faithful company throughout the project was my dog Lucky, a wheaten terrier. If Carlo comes to life as a character, I like to think that it is Lucky's gift to the book. The truth is, he slept through most of it.

ABOUT THE AUTHOR

James Sulzer, author of The Voice at the Door, lives on Nantucket Island, Massachusetts and teaches reading and writing to students in grades 5-8. A graduate of Yale University, where he was a Yale National Scholar, he is also the author of Nantucket Daybreak (Walker and Co.) and the memoir Mom Comes Home. He has produced countless "sonic id's" for National Public Radio, some of which aired on Ira Glass's This American Life. He has spent the past 40 years of his life reading, living with, and cherishing the poetry of Emily Dickinson.

SOURCES

All the poetry attributed to Emily Dickinson in this novel is from *The Poems of Emily Dickinson: Reading Edition,* Ralph W. Franklin, ed., Cambridge, Mass.: The Belknap Press of Harvard University Press, Copyright 1998, 1999 by the President and Fellows of Harvard College.

The only change I have made is in "The smouldering embers blush," where I have reverted to the original fascicle version for the last two lines. Significantly, the subsequent changes by Emily Dickinson were designed (in my opinion) to conceal the fact that the original referred to a beloved. She changed the original "This requisite has fire that lasts/It must at first be true" to the less forthcoming and rather elliptical "One requisite has fire that lasts/Prometheus never knew." With this poem, as with many others, Dickinson left a number of versions with no definitive word about which she preferred.

Excerpts from the sermons attributed to Charles Wadsworth are from the private collection of the Jones Library in Amherst.

For the enjoyment of the reader, I now list the portions of the poems of Emily Dickinson that appear in the novel, along with their designated numbers in *The Poems of Emily Dickinson: Reading Edition*, Ralph W. Franklin, ed.

p. 2, from "A Bird, came down the Walk" #359

> A Bird, came down the Walk –
> He did not know I saw –
> He bit an Angle Worm in halves
> And ate the fellow, raw

p. 3, from "A Bird, came down the Walk" #359

> They looked like frightened Beads . . .

p.3, from "A Bird, came down the Walk" #359

> He glanced with rapid eyes,
> That hurried all abroad –
> They looked like frightened Beads, I thought.

p. 5, from "I had been hungry, all the Years" #439

> I had been hungry, all the Years –
> My Noon had Come – to dine –

p. 30, from "A secret told" #643

> A Secret told –
> Ceases to be a Secret – then –

p. 57, from "Again his voice is at the door"#274

> Again – his voice is at the door –
> I feel the old Degree –
> I hear him ask the servant
> For such an one – as me . . .

p. 80, from "If you were coming in the Fall"#356

> If you were coming in the Fall,
> I'd brush the Summer by
> With half a smile, and half a spurn,
> As Housewives do, a Fly.
>
> If I could see you in a year,
> I'd wind the months in balls –
> And put them each in separate Drawers,
> For fear the numbers fuse –

p. 92, from "The Daisy follows soft the Sun" #161

> The Daisy follows soft the Sun –
> And when his golden walk is done –
> Sits Shily at his feet –
> He – waking – finds the flower there –
> Wherefore – Marauder – art thou here?
> Because, Sir, love is sweet!

p. 102, from "Title divine, is mine" #194

> Title divine, is mine.
> The Wife without the Sign –
> Acute Degree conferred on me –
> Empress of Calvary –
> Royal, all but the Crown –
> Betrothed, without the Swoon
> God gives us Women –
> When You hold Garnet to Garnet –
> Gold – to Gold –
> Born – Bridalled – Shrouded –
> In a Day –
> Tri Victory –
> "My Husband" – Women say
> Stroking the Melody –
> Is this the way –

p. 110, from "Rearrange a 'Wife's' Affection" #267

> Rearrange a "Wife's" Affection!
> When they dislocate my Brain!
> Amputate my freckled Bosom!
> Make me bearded like a man!
>
> Blush, my spirit, in thy Fastness –
> Blush, my unacknowledged clay –
> Seven years of troth have taught thee
> More than Wifehood ever may!

Love that never leaped it's socket –
Trust intrenched in narrow pain –
Constancy thro' fire – awarded –
Anguish – bare of anodyne!

Burden – borne so far triumphant –
None suspect me of the crown,
For I wear the "Thorns" till Sunset –
Then – my Diadem put on.

Big my Secret but it's bandaged –
It will never get away
Till the Day it's Weary Keeper
Leads it through the Grave to thee.

p. 114, from "The first Day's Night had come" #423

The first Day's Night had come –
And grateful that a thing
So terrible – had been endured –
I told my Soul to sing –

She said her strings were snapt –
Her bow – to atoms blown –
And so to mend her – gave me work
Until another Morn –

And then – a Day as huge
As Yesterdays in pairs,
Unrolled it's horror in my face –
Until it blocked my eyes . . .

p. 119, from "There is a pain – so utter –" #515

> There is a pain – so utter –
> It swallows substance up –
> Then covers the Abyss with Trance –
> So Memory can step
> Around – across – opon it –
> As One within a Swoon –
> Goes safely – where an open eye –
> Would drop Him – Bone by Bone –

p. 125, from "Dare you see a Soul at the "White Heat"? #401

> Dare you see a Soul at the "White Heat"?
> Then crouch within the door –
> Red – is the Fire's common tint –
> But when the vivid Ore
>
> Has vanquished Flame's conditions –
> It quivers from the Forge
> Without a color, but the Light
> Of unannointed Blaze –

p. 145, from "A wounded Deer – leaps highest –"#181

> A wounded Deer – leaps highest –
> I've heard the Hunter tell
> 'Tis but the extasy of death –
> And then the Brake is still!

p. 143, from "The smouldering embers blush" #1143

> The smouldering embers blush –
> Oh Heart within the Coal
> Hast thou survived so many years?
> The smouldering embers smile –
>
> Soft stirs the news of Light
> The stolid seconds glow
> This requisite has Fire that lasts
> It must at first be true –

p. 154, from "A Route of Evanescence" #1489

> A Route of Evanescence
> With a revolving Wheel –
> A Resonance of Emerald
> A Rush of Cochineal –
> And every Blossom on the Bush
> Adjusts it's tumbled Head –
> The Mail from Tunis – probably,
> An easy Morning's Ride –

p. 155, from "I shall not murmur if at last" #1429

> For what I shunned them so –
> Divulging it would rest my Heart
> But it would ravage theirs.

p. 155, from "Long years apart"#1405

> Long Years apart – can make no
> Breach a second cannot fill –
> The absence of the Witch does not
> Invalidate the spell –
>
> The embers of a Thousand Years
> Uncovered by the Hand
> That fondled them when they were Fire
> Will stir and understand.

p. 170, from "A Bird, came down the Walk"#359

> And he unrolled his feathers,
> And rowed him softer Home –
>
> Than Oars divide the Ocean,
> Too silver for a seam,
> Or Butterflies, off Banks of Noon,
> Leap, plashless as they swim.

READERS GUIDE

Questions for Discussion:

1) Did the portrayal of Emily Dickinson change your understanding of what she might have been like?

2) Did this novel change or deepen your understanding of the interplay and connection between Emily Dickinson's life and her poetry?

3) As a creative device do you think the story of the author finding his uncle's manuscript worked to frame the story effectively?

4) Describe the family dynamics of the Dickinson family as they are presented in this novel: Emily, her sister Vinnie, her brother Austin and his wife Susan, Father and Mother?

5) Emily Dickinson's relationship with her father has been the subject of much speculation. One school of thought believes that Edward Dickinson was an overbearing father who created a timid, reclusive child; other historians see a more nuanced and balanced relationship.

What view of the father-daughter relationship does this novel present? Did you find it believable?

6) This novel offers a new and controversial theory about a beloved American poet, introducing a medical reason (syphilis) that might have brought about her partial blindness in her early thirties as well as her subsequent reclusiveness.

a) How convincing was the syphilis theory for you?

b) Do you think that it was meant to be taken literally? Or (quoting the Afterword), was it meant more as a "literary conceit" — perhaps as a metaphor for the power and infectiousness of love?

7) How convincing was the novel in presenting an overwhelming, life-defining love between two people who saw each other only four or five times? How would you make sense today of a passion that encompassing?

8) Did you find Reverend Charles Wadsworth ultimately an admirable character, pious and important in the community, the opposite, or something in between?
Was this a believable portrayal?

9) The novel is framed by a single poem, "A Bird, came down the walk." The first four lines and some of the middle lines are quoted in the Prologue, and the final six lines are quoted at the end of the novel. You may want to read the poem in its entirety (#359 in Franklin's "Reading Edition").

a) Is the meeting between Emily Dickinson and the bird, as set forth in the poem—friendly, hesitant, or hostile?

b) Do you agree with the author about the perfection of Emily Dickinson's description of the look in a bird's eyes?

c) Also, do you think this poem was an appropriate one to use in framing the novel? Why or why not?

10) In what ways does the oppression of women account for who Emily Dickinson was and how she lived?

Questions for Discussion of Individual Poems

Several Emily Dickinson poems are quoted in their entirety in the novel. Here are some questions for discussion about three of them. Each poem is identified by its number in the R. W. Franklin "Reading Edition" of *The Poems of Emily Dickinson*.

"Title divine, is mine" #194

> Title divine, is mine.
> The Wife without the Sign –
> Acute Degree conferred on me –
> Empress of Calvary –
> Royal, all but the Crown –
> Betrothed, without the Swoon
> God gives us Women –
> When You hold Garnet to Garnet –
> Gold – to Gold –
> Born – Bridalled – Shrouded –
> In a Day –
> Tri Victory –
> "My Husband" – Women say
> Stroking the Melody –
> Is this the way –

If this verse is correctly dated, Emily Dickinson wrote this poem as Charles Wadsworth was preparing to move to San Francisco and be installed in the Calvary

Presbyterian Church. Some scholars believe that Dickinson used the word "Calvary" as a code name to stand for Wadsworth.

What do you think Emily Dickinson means by the lines, "Acute Degree conferred on me –/Empress of Calvary" and "Royal, all but the Crown –"?

"Rearrange a 'Wife's' Affection" #267

> Rearrange a "Wife's" Affection!
> When they dislocate my Brain!
> Amputate my freckled Bosom!
> Make me bearded like a man!
>
> Blush, my spirit, in thy Fastness –
> Blush, my unacknowledged clay –
> Seven years of troth have taught thee
> More than Wifehood ever may!
>
> Love that never leaped it's socket –
> Trust intrenched in narrow pain –
> Constancy thro' fire – awarded –
> Anguish – bare of anodyne!
>
> Burden – borne so far triumphant –
> None suspect me of the crown,
> For I wear the "Thorns" till Sunset –
> Then – my Diadem put on.

> Big my Secret but it's bandaged –
> It will never get away
> Till the Day it's Weary Keeper
> Leads it through the Grave to thee.

What do you think is the meaning of the last stanza? What is the "Secret"? Who is the "Weary Keeper"? Who is "thee"?

"There is a pain – so utter –" #515

> There is a pain – so utter –
> It swallows substance up –
> Then covers the Abyss with Trance –
> So Memory can step
> Around – across – opon it –
> As One within a Swoon –
> Goes safely – where an open eye –
> Would drop Him – Bone by Bone –

What do you think the first two lines mean: "There is a pain – so utter –/It swallows substance up –"?

What do you think it means when Dickinson writes: "Then covers the Abyss with Trance –/So Memory can step/Around – across – upon it –/As One within a Swoon –/Goes safely – "?

Fiction from Fuze Publishing

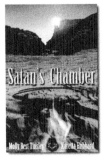

Satan's Chamber by Molly Best Tinsley and Karetta Hubbard

Her father was a crack CIA operative who vanished from the streets of Khartoum, Sudan. Victoria Pierce joins the Agency to learn why. From the minute she's posted to this rogue state, nothing is what it seems. Spy thriller.

The Mother Daughter Show by Natalie Wexler

At a D.C. prep school so elite its parent body includes the President and First Lady—three mothers have thrown themselves into organizing the annual musical revue. Will its Machiavellian intrigue somehow enable them to reconnect with their graduating daughters, who are fast spinning out of control?

Black Wings by Kathleen Jabs

Lieutenant Bridget Donovan battles Navy hierarchy to find the truth behind the tragic plane crash of one of the Navy's first female combat pilots, Audrey Richards, Bridget's Academy roommate. Bridget's life is at stake when she uncovers the warped code of honor behind a secret Academy group. Mystery.

Cologne by Sarah Pleydell

London, 1960. Renate von Has-selmann, an au pair escaping postwar Germany, takes charge of precocious Caroline and Maggie Whitaker. The girls' debonair father disarms the young woman with his quicksilver charm, childhood collides with history, and the traumas of war are visited upon the children of the peace.

Leaving Tuscaloosa by Walter Bennett

1962. Racial turmoil in the deep South engulfs two estranged boyhood friends, one black and one white. Veering from the heat of erotic passion to the spreading fires of racial violence, their paths converge in a moving, shocking climax.

Broken Angels by Molly Best Tinsley

Under deep cover in Odessa, Ukraine, Victoria Pierce is tasked with confirming the secret export of highly enriched uranium from Ukraine's stockpiles. When she collides with a girl on the run from sex traffickers, she finds herself enmeshed in a sticky web of vice that extends to dangerously high places.

Pepperoni Palm Tree by Aidan Patrick Meath and Jason Killian Meath

When a boy meets the only pepperoni palm tree in the world, both face the challenge of being true to oneself in a story that celebrates the uniqueness that enables each of us to shine, and thus enlighten the world. Children's Fiction.

Memoir from Fuze Publishing

The Gift of El Tio by Larry Buchanan and Karen Gans

When world-renowned geologist discovers an enormous deposit of silver beneath a remote Quechua village in Bolivia, he unknowingly fulfills a 450-year-old prophecy that promised a life of wealth for the villagers.

Nobody Knows the Spanish I Speak by Mark Saunders

High-tech couple from Portland, Oregon, emigrates with large dog and ornery cat to San Miguel de Allende, in the middle of Mexico. Their well-intentioned cluelessness makes for mayhem and non-stop laughs.

Entering the Blue Stone by Molly Best Tinsley

The General battles Parkinson's; his wife manifests a bizarre dementia. Their grown children embrace what seems a solution--an upscale retirement community. Between laughter and dismay, discover what shines beneath catastrophe: family bonds, the dignity of even an unsound mind, and the endurance of the heart.

How the Winds Laughed by Addie Greene

When Addie Greene and her young husband take on the "great adventure" of circumnavigation in a 28-foot boat, a succession of catastrophes demands that she become the driving force in carrying them forward and safely home.

CPSIA information can be obtained at www.ICGtesting.com
Printed in the USA
LVOW05s2229141014

408810LV00013B/291/P

9 780989 730624